LUKE RICHARDSON

Hong Kong

Chapter 1

Looking back, Jamie wished it had never happened.

He thumped so hard against the window of time, hoping that his previous self would hear the warning. But nothing changed. The night, unedited, scrolled through his mind, the same events, leading to the same result, leading to the same events, leading to now.

Opening his eyes slowly, he hoped things would be different. They weren't.

The dark cell, the smell of strong disinfectant, the swirling lights through the dirty glass above his bed. Someone on his block shouting – "No! No! No!" – louder with each repetition.

In his head the memory of the night restarts.

Isobel shivers like the last fruit of the forbidden tree. Delectable, vulnerable, obtainable. She leans against the railing of the bar they're in, her bare shoulders slightly hunched against the evening's chill.

He hasn't noticed how beautiful she is before. Or maybe he has but just hasn't thought about it.

London lies in front of her, relaxing into the evening. It's as though even the city knows what's going to happen and can't do anything about it. Isobel traces the routes of the taxis below with her fingertips. Slender pale fingers, long red nails.

Being ten floors up is enough to make you feel detached from the world; you can watch it without being part of it.

Isobel straightens up. Maybe she's heard Jamie's footsteps joining her on the balcony. Maybe it's the chill of the evening. She moves her right arm around the back of her long, straight, red hair and sweeps it over her shoulder. It falls down her chest, curving over her shoulder, past the swell of her breasts beneath the strapless red dress.

From the door to the balcony, Jamie waits, considering his move. He's had enough drinks to disregard concerns about sleeping with a colleague. How to make it happen, that's his concern now.

Inside the party flows. Flashing lights and dancing. Jackets and ties are abandoned as people stomp to the music.

Jamie walks towards her. He lets her hear his footsteps. He wants her to hear his footsteps, so she'll know it's him.

"The city really does look beautiful from here, doesn't it?" he asks, joining her on the railing. Their elbows touch imperceptibly.

"Yeah," she says, turning to look at him. "What's that over there?" she asks, pointing towards the flashing needle of The Shard.

"You've been here long enough to know that."

"Nearly six months." She turns to face him.

"Where did you live before?"

"A long way from here." She exhales deeply, her breath is a wisp in the cold night. "Are you playing the game too?"

The game? Jamie thinks, confused. *Maybe she's not that innocent after all.*

"The one where you pretend to be enjoying yourself. This totally isn't your scene."

2

Jamie laughs to himself. *This IS going to be easy. She'll talk herself into it.*

The rumble of celebration continues from the bar. The DJ plays a tune the swelling crowd agree with. There's a cheer and singing.

Jamie says nothing. The city turns in its sleep.

She'll talk herself into this. They always do.

"I like this place," Isobel says, filling the silence.

Let her do the work. She's committed.

Jamie turns to look at her, saying nothing.

She wants to talk.

"It's a nice bar, don't you think? It's peaceful up here."

Silence will make her want it more.

"I've not been before." Jamie appeases the question. He's not been because it's tacky. Neon and chrome.

They both stare out towards nothing. Isobel shivers and slides towards him on the railing.

"Parties like this can be crazy, though. Sometimes I don't even know what the point is. Everyone's drunk and most don't even like each other."

Jamie notices her voice softening with alcohol. He's heard her in the office, although they've never spoken personally.

"You've got to enjoy yourself, or you're fired," Jamie says without looking at her.

A champagne cork cracks in the distance.

"I'm not sure," she replies. "I'll run that past Tony." Behind them the managing director staggers around the bar, pouring champagne into people's mouths.

Let's speed this up.

"I'm not sure he'd really care right now." Jamie turns to face her, sliding his right hand to the small of her back.

3

Something thumps from the door. Two women Jamie recognizes from Finance. He watches them over Isobel's head as they rummage through handbags for a lighter, cigarettes bobbing between rosed lips.

They would be way too easy, although a worthy back-up.

Focusing on Isobel, Jamie watches the smile breed across her lips. Neither move. Jamie takes in her height, her complexion, the sensual shape of her back. Looking down past her gaze, he watches the strapless dress sink lower.

It'll look good on the floor later.

The moment rests as though drunk. Silence.

Isobel moves, now she's pushing towards him. He can feel her body enticing him.

There's a thump again in the distance, lost in the swirl of the city.

Her right hand moves to his left arm, his left to her thigh.

Jamie leans in and kisses her. He's done this before.

Behind the one-way screen of memory, Jamie thumps and cries. But it makes no difference. Nothing changes.

He leans in and kisses her.

He's done it now, set himself on the path to the smell of disinfectant, the echoing cries of other men and the swirling lights of captivity.

Chapter 2

Leo ran, he always ran. It made him feel good. It revitalized and energized him. He ran along Brighton's sea front, as though taking in the world for the first time.

When Leo had a normal job and kept normal hours he would run before work. He would leave his flat, two streets back at the Hove end of the town and run as far as time would allow. Now a man of his own destiny, his own lord, boss and master, he ran when he wanted. Usually around lunchtime he would find himself pulling tight the laces on his faded red trainers and heading down to the seafront.

It was one of those spring days where the world finally seemed to crawl out from hibernation, yawn and sit up a little. The sky was bright and cloudless, the air still. The seagulls were working hard to fly without the currents of wind which had embattled the city for the last few months. Pushing his headphones in a little tighter, Leo tried to dull their mournful, swooping cries.

To his right, the stones of the beach ran down to the water. Emerging from the winter, they were banked in swathes at Nature's whim. Soon, men with diggers would come and level it all out again - the constant battle to undo the effects of nature.

It was entropy, a word Leo had recently learned watching a TV documentary. Entropy – as far as he understood – was nature's ability to spread things around, return everything to disorder. Disorder was simple. Disorder was easy.

It was order and organization that was difficult. That's where the challenge was, and that was where he now made his money. Despite nature's want to separate, spread and settle, people like Leo fought to find and reunite. He seemed to be good at it.

Pounding the pavements in the still afternoon air, he let the thoughts drift from his mind. Mental entropy – if that was a term. Leo thought it should be. He let things go, settle, spread.

Ahead, Brighton seafront's endless row of terraced hotels ran to nothing. Some of them gleamed, fresh and new, others grey and tired. Rugged scaffold towers had started to appear in front of those being spruced up for the summer, juxtaposing the waving bay windows and black ironwork. To his right, the column of the newly opened i360 observation tower sparkled in the bright sunlight.

Leo was pleased to get his fitness back. Six months ago, he had returned from a long working holiday feeling flabby and out of shape. He couldn't even make it down to the seafront without a strain. Now, if there wasn't much he needed to do in the afternoon, he could run as far as the Pavilion and back.

Things had been crazy since returning. His life had been transformed. He'd inadvertently found a new calling, one he hadn't even thought possible less than a year ago. It had all happened so quickly he didn't even know what the job was called. One of the magazines that interviewed him called him an International Missing Persons Investigator, but that sounded far too self-important. Leo was only doing what he could to help people that needed it.

It wasn't all good though, he thought, noticing the monolithic Grand Hotel up ahead. That's where it all started less than a year ago. Before visiting the hotel, Leo didn't know anything about Kathmandu, or Allissa, or Blake Stockwell. Now he shuddered at the name.

Fortunately, they had missed most of Scotland Yard's investigation by extending their time away. Although they were warned on their return that it would be easy for a powerful and wealthy man to arrange some kind of consequence.

"Be vigilant, look what's around you, stay safe, and call me if you need anything," a detective from Scotland Yard had said, handing Leo a card. After that, Leo saw danger everywhere. A woman with a red hat changing her mind in the supermarket was someone doubling back to follow him. Two passing black cars in the same day was a possible kidnap attempt. A man on the phone was someone watching him, waiting for their time to strike.

After two nights lying awake waiting for the door to be broken down, and the third time searching the flat for recording devices, Leo decided enough was enough and moved into a hotel for a few days.

Things had got better since Stockwell was charged. Then when he was sentenced and sent to prison, Leo started to feel safe again.

Now, Leo tried to run as often as possible, but the work was demanding. In the last six months he had gone away three times, once for over three weeks. With that in mind, it was a victory every time he made it out in the rain or shine.

He would have to turn around soon, he had a busy afternoon. A client was trying to get him to go to Edinburgh to find her son who had disappeared with his girlfriend.

"We never liked her anyway," the woman said by way of explanation when they had spoken on the phone.

For Leo, the challenge was now deciding which cases he wanted to take. Many people offered to pay him, but he knew the work was hard, time-consuming and unfortunately, in many circumstances, fruitless. After six months of daily requests, he was having to say no to those that he thought were better suited for someone else.

For the Edinburgh case, Leo was talking to a local private detective who he hoped would do the legwork for him, meaning he shouldn't have to leave Brighton at all.

Back at the flat, Leo got straight to work; he'd change later. A run always got him fired up, ready to make things happen.

Shaking the mouse, the two screens of his computer flickered to life. Behind them, through the bay window of his top floor flat, the slate rooftops ran down to the sea somewhere beyond.

Leo had been tempted to move from the tatty flat when work started going well. But with the increasingly small amounts of time he spent there, he didn't see the need. Plus, in many ways he liked it, or at least was used to it.

Re-reading one of the e-mails from the lady whose son had supposedly fled to Edinburgh, Leo began to compose a message to his contact there. The more information he could pass on the better.

Enthralled in the process, copying words from one page to the next, Leo didn't hear the footsteps climbing the stairs. Leo had to get this right. If this model worked, his business could be viable. He could work from his flat and move around the world with the speed and agility of an e-mail, but it had to be done correctly.

Leo didn't hear the door behind him swing open either. Nor did he notice the footsteps start to cross the room.

It just has to be done right, Leo thought as the intruder came closer.

Chapter 3

J amie hates Monday mornings. As a man who enjoys his weekend, Monday signals a return to drudgery and imprisonment. To him it seems as though the colour of the world starts to drain on a Sunday afternoon. Only a sepia tone wreckage of responsibility and regret remains by the time the alarm sounds on Monday morning.

It's alright though, he reminds himself, slipping from the car and into the office's damp smelling car park, he's leaving soon.

He's not just leaving though he thinks, stepping into the lift, pressing the button for the sixth floor and waiting for the doors to close. He's not just replacing one tired firm with another. He's not even leaving to set up his own firm of architects. Jamie is going to Hong Kong.

Ever since completing the drawn-out education process students of architecture must endure, Jamie has wanted to travel. Although his thirst for adventure has been sated a couple of times with extended holidays to Asia, South America and the Far East, his real aim has always been to live in and help design one of the world's leading cities. An afternoon spent walking between the crystal-glass towers of Hong Kong's financial district three years ago put the city firmly on his list.

Jamie knows he's been lucky to have worked on some exciting projects in London, but there's only ever going to be so much you can do in such a sprawling and historical city. In London, each square inch is owned, legislated and accounted for. Hong Kong is different. There's opportunity, excitement and the ability to play with the city in ways he wouldn't get elsewhere. The opportunity to design buildings that truly inspire. The Burj, Shanghai Tower, Taipei 101. The sort of buildings that cause people to stand in the street open-mouthed, gawping skywards. Testaments to human will, creativity and power.

Two weeks. Just two weeks and he'll be off.

There's no sound that represents the lifestyle of the battery human better than the 'mail received' tone Jamie hears as he opens his laptop. Sitting down, he starts to scroll through the messages; he'll need a coffee before getting on with any real work.

He deletes four e-mails straight off, forwards two to his P.A. to be actioned, and stops to read the last.

Isobel Clarke

Sunday morning, 10:13

Last night was so nice, it was a shame you had to leave early. It wasn't until you'd gone I realised I don't have your number. Spending the night together was great. It turned out to be a pretty good party in the end.

Jamie loses focus on the e-mail as he remembers the evening. It had been good.

The events turn hazily through his mind. Kissing on the balcony. Hands exploring. The red dress slipping lower. Isobel's head falling backwards as he kisses down her neck.

Kissing against the mirrored wall of the hotel lift. A dozen reflected versions of themselves doing the same. Then finally, in the room, pushing the red dress to the floor. The hunter and the hunted.

Isobel was ambitious, confident and keen - he could tell that by what happened next. It's true, he had noticed her around the office a few times. She had worked on the interiors team.

The memory made him grin as he regained focus on the e-mail.

I'll come and see you later.

Isobel xxx

This certainly couldn't happen. He couldn't be having a relationship with someone on the team. He was leaving.

Jamie would have to make that clear.

He didn't have to wait long.

"So, this is where you're hiding?" A voice from the door of his office, sharp, demanding. Isobel.

Jamie looks up from the redesign of the council offices in Brentwood he's working on. If he smiles, it's nerves. Gone is the softness of the alcohol and the evening. The red hair which had flowed across his pillow is now pinned aggressively high.

"Saturday was good. We totally need to talk about when it'll happen again."

She moves forwards, puts her hands on the desk and leans towards Jamie as though expecting him to kiss her. He doesn't. Although he does get a view down her top.

Jamie considers his words carefully. In the silence he hears noise from the outside office. Indistinct conversations, the rattle of keyboards. Somewhere a kettle nears its boiling point.

"Yeah, Saturday was... nice. It was nice. But, yeah, I don't want you to get the wrong impression… We'd both had a lot to drink."

Jamie's computer pings, he ignores it, keeping eye contact. Damage limitation.

Isobel steps back as though breathless.

"But those things…" Isobel says.

Jamie tries to push the memories from his mind. The red dress falling to the floor.

"The things you said…"

The kettle continues to boil unnoticed.

Did he say anything that could have given her the wrong idea? Jamie can't remember. He thinks better than pointing that out.

"We were so close!" Isobel says bitterly.

Jamie suppresses an unexpected smirk and closes the conversation down.

"Yeah, I'm sorry. I was really drunk - it was great fun though… thanks."

Was the 'thanks' too far?

Isobel's complexion reddens. Her eyes swell. Jaw locked and eyebrows tense.

"I definitely shouldn't have bothered – fuck you!" she hisses, turns and walks from the office.

The mail received tone sounds from Jamie's computer again, but he isn't looking. He's watching Isobel, her ass wiggling from the room.

She did look good naked.

On the screen an e-mail from his colleague in the next office waits.

You're a dickhead, Jamie! ;)

The lights thump to life; time for the five hundred or so

13

men on Jamie's wing to get up. Even though it's barely light outside, Jamie doesn't mind getting up. It makes a change from staring at the ceiling alone with his thoughts. He hasn't slept properly in weeks. This nightmare has no escape.

Chapter 4

Allissa tried to resist the urge to giggle as she tiptoed up behind Leo. It was hilarious how jumpy he got. It was especially hilarious a few months ago. The idea that he stayed in a hotel for a week because he was too scared to go home cracked her up. I mean, the guy was in prison, what was he going to do from there?

"If they were going to do anything, they would have done it in Kathmandu," she'd said. "Everyone's got eyes on him now and he knows it. He won't be able to get near you, or get anyone to."

After the sentencing, she thought Leo's anxiety about it would probably stop. For the benefit of her own amusement, if nothing else, it hadn't.

It had been strange for Allissa to watch Blake Stockwell receive his sentence. They had been there, Leo and her, in the court that day. It was strange because, despite what he had done to her, her mother and to other people, he was still her father. She still had memories of his kindness. Sometimes he had even been a good father. Loving and attentive. The man she watched receiving his sentence in court that day didn't seem like him at all.

Allissa knew this was justice. He had – whether in sound

15

mind or not (a defence his lawyer had suggested but had been quickly rejected) – tried to have her and Leo killed in Kathmandu. He had bribed immigration officials to keep her mother from entering the country, forcefully separated their family, and ultimately, conspired to have her murdered. There was a whole file of other bribery, extortion and conspiratorial claims going back decades which lawyers were still trying to understand.

But as Allissa had watched him that day – looking slimmer, tired and older than the man he had been before she went away – she could only remember the happy times. How they'd played on the giant rug in the family room on a Saturday afternoon when she was little. Long walks through fields and woods; his knowledge of wildlife had always been excellent. The feeling of coming back home from university, knowing he'd be there to talk about her studies and her life.

That man was gone now.

The shrivelled, pink-faced man whose clothes hung from him didn't look like her father at all.

So, creeping up behind Leo in the front room, it was funny that he'd still jump so much. Approaching the desk, Allissa cowered over him ready to pounce.

Two steps away.

One step away.

"Raaah!" Leo shouted, catching her by surprise and spinning around in his chair. Allissa jumped and squealed, moving just out of the way as he made a grab for her.

"How did you…" Allissa said though the laughter. Then she noticed, stuck to the corner of the computer screen, a small mirror showing a reflection of the room behind him. He'd have seen her all the way.

Leo may be easy to scare but he was always well-prepared. Maybe that's what made them a good team.

Chapter 5

"...And that should see our pre-tax profits for the quarter increase by over five percent," drones Mr Beige in front of a screen displaying a graph with an upward curving blue line. From the back-row Jamie stifles a yawn.

Who is this prick trying to impress? Anyone can draw a graph.

It's a general staff meeting in the big conference room. Thirty or so people. One of the partners discussing some new legislation Jamie doesn't know or care about. He's leaving.

Jamie checks his watch again – thirty-five minutes. He's already considered in detail each of the mass-produced water-colours hanging on the walls of the room. Each inoffensive, but devoid of character and personality. A metaphor for the man who continues to talk from the front perhaps.

"Just to reiterate that, I know you've heard it before but..."

Jamie notices Isobel sitting in the front row, listening attentively. Her hair wobbles with each nod of agreement. They haven't spoken in a week, since the discussion. She's been working hard to ignore him.

"Thanks for that, Carl," the Managing Director interrupts before the third repetition.

"Some more good news – it's an exciting time to work here." He gets to his feet and faces the assembled staff. "We're all very lucky to be part of such a dynamic, forward-thinking company…"

Jamie notices Isobel nodding with renewed energy as he tunes out again.

"…but because we are so forward thinking and aspirational for ourselves and each other, members of our family do sometimes leave us for exciting new opportunities. With the confidence and skills they have gained working here…"

He's not going to… is he… please no…

Jamie's suddenly alert, a sickening feeling rising.

"Jamie, who has been working with us for nearly three years now," the MD says, catching Jamie's eyes and extending a hand towards him, "will be leaving to take a very exciting opportunity in Hong Kong. It'll be sad for us to see him go, but Jamie, we wish you the best of luck."

Heads turn towards him, most contorted into smiles of congratulation.

One unabashed scowl.

Meeting adjourned.

Jamie smiles in thanks and heads for the door. There goes the chances of him sneaking out quietly on his last day.

"Why didn't you tell me?" He knows the owner of the voice before he sees them. He doesn't reply.

"Well? Didn't you think I had a right to know?"

Isobel. She stands there, just outside the door to the conference room – as though waiting for him.

"After all that's happened, you didn't have an ounce of decency in you to tell me?" Hands on hips, eyes boring into his. They're green, Jamie notices for the first time.

It's really none of her business, Jamie thinks, stopping himself from saying it. He doesn't want to make things more difficult than necessary.

"I bet you think it's none of my business..."

"Well... I..." Jamie stutters.

"You're wrong. I have a right to know these things. When were you planning to let me know this little scheme of yours?"

Why does she care? Why is she even talking to me?

"Well I'm telling you now," Isobel says, "it's not happening. You can tell everyone you want, whatever you want, but you're not going."

Jamie stands in the corridor and watches Isobel walk away, his mind filling with clever and witty responses he'll never get to say.

Go. Get out of there, Jamie screams at himself from the lumpy bed.

Leave the place and don't go back. Go now.

But his voice just echoes from the bare brick walls and nothing changes.

Chapter 6

"Thinking you can sneak up on me, huh?" Leo shouted, tickling Allissa who roared with laughter.

"You're just too easy to…"

"Too easy to what?"

"Alright, alright!" Allissa said stepping out of reach and turning to face him.

Their eyes connected for a moment. Leo felt a flush rising across his cheeks and turned back toward the computer. Drawing a deep breath, he tried to regain focus on the screen.

"What are you doing here?" Allissa asked, moving in close behind him. Leo took another slow breath.

Clearing his throat, Leo explained how he was trying to get things moving between the client and the detective he'd found in Edinburgh. Then neither of them would need to leave Brighton.

"Sounds good," Allissa said, crossing the room, sitting on the sofa and starting the laptop which sat amid papers on the coffee table.

"I'll have a sort through some of those e-mails. Still got those invoices to do."

Leo and Allissa had been working together since returning from Nepal a few months ago. At first, neither were sure about it – the memories of Kathmandu were all too close and shocking – but with the publicity they got through Stockwell's prosecution, the pair realised how many people needed their help.

So, they'd cleared out the second bedroom in Leo's flat, bought some new furniture and started living and working together.

The front room had changed too. Leo had taken down the map around which the leads on his still-missing ex-girlfriend had been displayed. They were still in a file in his room somewhere, but he didn't need to see them everyday anymore. He'd even stopped the search program which had grown ever more fruitless and random over the three years since she'd disappeared. If they were meant to find each other again, Leo had thought, then they would. He couldn't spend his whole life looking.

Turning and looking at Allissa, a thought occurred to Leo.

"What are you doing this weekend?"

"Nothing really," she said, looking up at him, "I said I'd work on that update for the website we've needed for a while, re-write a load of the old 'how-to' guides."

Leo nodded. Allissa's impact on the Missing People International site was significant; she was far better at marketing and design than he was. At least half of the enquiries they now got and the money they made was the result of Allissa's work.

"You can't work all weekend. Why don't you come with me tomorrow?"

"What to your sister's?"

"Yeah, it'll be fun. I've rented a car, we'll drive down, have a few drinks, stay the night then come back on Sunday."

Allissa looked thoughtfully.

"You need some time away from this place," Leo said.

"You're asking if I want to come to your sister's with you?" Allissa said, tilting her head and examining Leo closely.

"Yeah…"

"To get me out of the house?"

"Well, yeah."

"Just say you want me to come for back-up then," she said, her dark eyes showing the smile her face was trying to hide.

"Yes, totally," Leo laughed. "Got it in one."

"Sure, I'll come," Allissa said. "They can't be as crazy as my family."

Chapter 7

Friday night. One week to go until Jamie leaves for good.

Flights are booked and the company he'll be working for have sent him pictures of the apartment. It looks amazing. Ten stories up, floor-to-ceiling windows. A balcony looking out across Kowloon and beyond.

Waiting for the lift down to the office car park, he counts the days he has left. Five working days. It almost feels achievable. He can do this.

Avoiding Isobel for the last couple of weeks hasn't been easy. He's had to get in early and stay late each night. People must think it's a last-ditch attempt to get a good reference, but it's anything to avoid talking to her again.

Just need to get out.

The lift doors slide open revealing the car park's smell of damp.

Just get out now.

The office car park is a dank, low-ceilinged basement beneath the building. Most people rely on public transport, so it's not often used and as such badly maintained. Jamie, having already let his flat, has been driving from his parents' house in Woking each day.

His footsteps echo as he walks into the darkness. Only half the lights work and the gate to the street is never locked making it a great place for anyone with nowhere better to go. The combined smell of petrol and piss turns his stomach.

Jamie doesn't see the shape standing near his car until he's a few steps away. When he does, he doesn't know what it is. He just knows that it's not usually there.

"Hello?" he asks the darkness, he'll look crazy if it's nothing. "Hello, are you okay?"

It's probably a drunk sheltering from the rain. Just get in the car.

Hearing the voice, Jamie knows who it is.

"I don't know how you can do it."

It's the voice of nightmares. Isobel.

She moves from the shadow towards his car. Orange light falls violently across her face.

"I just don't know how you can do it."

Jamie wants to walk away more than anything. He can't. She's standing in front of his car.

"I really don't know what you mean. I'm just trying to get home."

Just get in the car and go.

"How can you just walk around here like nothing's happened, like you haven't done anything?" Her voice is sharper than usual, shaking, hoarse, desperate.

Jamie rubs the bridge of his nose between finger and thumb.

"I'm sorry if you feel I've upset you by not telling you – if you feel I've led you on," Jamie says softly. He needs to talk her away from the car and get going. "You're a really nice person. It's just, you know, I'm leaving. If I wasn't, I'd definitely want to see you again."

25

"You! I wouldn't want to see you if you were the last person in the world! You make me sick!" Isobel's shouting now.

She steps forward, towards him.

Jamie looks around, hoping to see someone else come down the stairs. Any distraction to get him past her and into the car.

"What's the problem then?" he says aggressively. He's had enough. This girl is crazy. He'll call in on Monday and just say that he can't come in. Screw the reference, it's not worth this.

"Isobel, I'm going to get in my car now and go home."

The car beeps as he presses the key remote in his pocket.

Walking past her, Jamie pulls the door open.

Don't look up. Don't engage with her. Just go home.

Her next comment drops like a bomb. The sort that ruins lives.

"I just don't remember giving you consent."

It sounds almost tearful, resentful, believable. It's clearly not true. She kissed him. She definitely kissed him.

Jamie stares at her. His jaw feels slack. The thud of a passing truck rumbles through the car park.

"You can't be saying that. That's completely untrue and you know it!"

Anger builds.

How can she say that? What's she trying to do?

"I just can't remember." She's sobbing now. The silhouette of her shoulders pulse as she breathes, "I want to remember, Jamie, but I can't, I can't… You did this."

"Don't say that, Isobel. It's not true… It's not true and you know it."

Tight chested, straight backed, fight or flight.

A light flits into the darkness from the other side of the car park. Isobel's expression changes. She's smiling. Smiling through the tears. She fixes Jamie in her gaze. A cat playing with its prey. Lifting her left hand, she holds a folded piece of paper towards him.

"That's my address," she says, her voice normal again. All trace of distress is gone. "Come at nine and our secret will stay that way."

Chapter 8

Leo enjoyed the drive to Yatton, the village in North Somerset where his sister Emma lived with her husband and three-year-old son. Although diligently learning to drive as a teenager, Leo had never owned a car. Having spent most of his life in the city, he felt there was never the need. He had, however, rented one for the weekend so he, and now Allissa, could make the three-hour journey in comfort.

The previous night, at the rental place, Leo had been faced with the choice of a small Toyota, or for an extra £25 a BMW 1 Series. Now, powering past two lorries, feeling the grumble of the engine, he didn't regret his decision.

Along the banks of the motorway, signs of spring pushed themselves skyward. Green shoots flowered into blue, yellow and white with the warmer weather. The harsh blue of the late morning sky was cloudless behind skeletal trees.

Emma, Andy and Frankie had moved into their new house around the same time Leo and Allissa had returned from Kathmandu. Although Leo had seen them at his parents in Bath, he'd not made it to their new place yet, much to his sister's disapproval. It seemed that now Emma had four-bedrooms, she felt the obligation to fill them as frequently as possible. In reality, it was not a prospect Leo savoured. Firstly, it was a long journey. Secondly, Frankie loved to fill the house with the noise of shouting and crashing furniture. And finally, despite trying on multiple occasions, Leo really didn't find Emma's husband Andy good company at all. In fact, he found the man simply infuriating.

With the thought, Leo felt frustration prickle across his skin and a growing desire to turn around and go home. He took a deep breath. On the passenger seat next to him, Allissa slept. Snatching a glance at her as he pulled into the inside lane, Leo felt his anger subside and a smile begin to form. No, he would go to see his sister. He would do the good big brother thing and, if needed, he would stand up to Andy.

Chapter 9

Jamie's drive home passes in a blur. The city streaks in neon scars against the rain-flecked windows.

He shouldn't go, he'd be mad to, right? He should stay away from her.

But what if she says that?

What if she says that he forced himself upon her? Or worse that she said no and that he had been too drunk to listen?

As he slows to a wash of red taillights ahead, Jamie knows he would never do that. Even the thought of it shocks him. He hadn't with Isobel. She'd been consenting alright. She'd wanted it as much as he had, he was sure of it. The way she'd kissed him, the things she'd done.

But the allegation itself could ruin him, there's no way the company in Hong Kong would still want him with this hanging over him. He needs to resolve it.

As the traffic pulls away, inching its way out of the city, Jamie slides the window down. The night's heavy, threatening and morose. Jamie knows everything hangs in the balance. He must solve it. He has to. Outside, through the open window, he feels anticipation in the air. Something's going to happen. Taking a deep breath of it, Jamie makes a decision.

Chapter 10

Allissa woke as the car slowed. Through the window the scene had changed. When she'd closed her eyes the banks of the motorway were speeding past, now they were crawling into a modern housing estate. Gleaming houses seemed to spring from both sides of the road, each slightly different and set at varying angles. The lawns of the houses reached down to the roadside, some already littered with pesky wildflowers. A light aeroplane skipped through the sky; the drone of its motor inaudible through the window. Allissa yawned.

"Hey, she's awake, thanks for the company," Leo said. "Had a really nice chat."

"Are we there?" Allissa squinted towards him.

"Yeah, I think. I hope so. It's number fifteen."

Allissa nestled back into her hoody and stretched. It was warm inside the car, but through the glass the world looked cold. While travelling she hadn't missed the British winters. During the two years she had been away she'd always managed to find herself a warm country for the winter months. Allissa liked the warmth, she felt good in it. She could wear bright clothes and didn't have to worry about cumbersome coats or scarves. Even with mosquitoes and cockroaches, Allissa knew she'd take a hot climate any day. She was half-African after all.

"That's it," Leo said, pulling the car to the kerb outside number fifteen.

Allissa didn't reply but shivered in anticipation of him opening the door.

"Thank you for coming," Leo said. "I think you'll find it… enlightening."

"I'm considering it an investigation, like Louis Theroux, undercover."

"Good idea," Leo cut the engine and sounded the horn. "Here we go."

"It'll be fine."

"It'll be fine for you," Leo opened the door. "They're my family, you're just here for the food."

They really can't be that bad, Allissa thought, shivering with the invasion of cold.

"So good to see you," Emma squealed from the open door as Allissa followed Leo towards the house. "Welcome, oh this is so nice."

As Emma squeezed Leo into a hug, Allissa couldn't help but notice how different they looked. Emma was dainty and feminine with long blonde hair and pale skin. She was glamourous and well-kept. Leo looked scruffy by comparison with his messy hair and baggy clothes. But then Allissa knew she didn't look like her brother and sister either.

"Oh, you've brought someone with you," Emma said.

"Yeah sorry, I should have said. We only decided late last night."

Leo made the introductions.

"Men, hey," Emma said, hugging Allissa and punching Leo

playfully on the arm, "they're rubbish at these sorts of things."

"Tell me about it," Allissa replied.

"Well let's show you the place," Emma said turning and leading them inside.

To Allissa, used to Leo's flat and before that moving frequently from place to place, the house looked unused. It certainly didn't look like the residence of a three-year-old. Following Emma into the large kitchen, gleaming in tile and chrome, Emma introduced Andy.

"Alright pal, how are you?" Andy said, finishing his bottle of beer and shaking Leo's hand.

"Yeah, alright."

Noticing Allissa, Andy's small eyes narrowed and he pulled Leo in close. Allissa didn't hear what he said but saw Leo shake his head in tense irritation as he pulled away.

Watching the pair, Allissa noticed there were two empty beer bottles on the counter already.

"Would you like something to drink?" Emma asked.

"Sure," Allissa said automatically. "I'll have a beer."

"Get me one an' all," Andy said, "and Leo too."

As Emma opened the fridge, a sibilant female voice came from the hallway.

"Where's this brother of yours then?"

Leo turned in confusion and caught Allissa's eye.

"I've been looking forward to meeting him all morning."

Chapter 11

At ten past nine, Jamie pulls up outside Isobel's apartment block. They're the sort of modern apartments that are thrown together on landfill sites and sold for a fortune. Outside, a row of Audis and BMWs glimmer beneath the orange sky of the city.

Sitting in the car, Jamie looks up at the outline of the building.

This is a crazy idea. He should be anywhere but here.

Twice he changes his mind. Once he even starts the car.

He's got to go in. This can't happen. He'll go in, reason with her, apologise and then leave. Then he's done everything he can.

At the first sign of her getting crazy, I'm out of there.

At least if she makes allegations now, he can say he's tried everything.

I'll be in Hong Kong soon, Jamie mutters to himself, getting out of the car, the cold stinging his face. *This will just be a bad memory.*

"Come up, third floor, flat 319," says the voice of nightmares on the intercom, followed by the buzz of the door.

The corridor is stark against the grim darkness outside. The sort of bright light which makes you feel dirty, as though it's exposing your secrets. Jamie passes the lift. He doesn't want to have to wait for it and if he needs to leave in a hurry he needs to know where the stairs are.

This is such a bad idea.

Go in, reason with her, and leave.

Each landing is the same. Behind each door someone's Friday night plays out. There's the faint sound of music and laughter as someone in a flat nearby prepares for a celebration.

Flat 319 is quiet.

Jamie knocks. Waits. If he thinks about it now, he'll turn, leave and won't come back.

Maybe that would be for the best.

The lock clicks as it disengages. The door opens. Isobel.

Jamie doesn't know what he was expecting, but this wasn't it.

The woman who opens the door hardly looks like Isobel at all – but it is her. All the meanness is gone. She looks scared, timid, meek. Her red hair, usually so close to perfect, is down and messed up at one side. Her green eyes are shot with red and framed with a blotchy, pale complexion. She's wearing a white and pink dressing gown – the sort Jamie has seen on the back of many girls' bedroom doors. Isobel's is faded, even in the half-light.

Where's the vicious tongue, dirty looks and shocking, perfect hair?

Isobel looks up at him and moves aside, allowing him in. He hesitates for a second. This is his last chance to go back.

Down the corridor a neighbour leaves their flat. The door behind them bangs as they head for the lift. Looking back, they notice Jamie at Isobel's door. It's a look that lingers. Remembering the details.

It'll be those details that seal Jamie's sentence.

Isobel beckons him in. The door closes behind him.

Inside the apartment's a mess. Burglars would take more care than she has.

Clothes and shoes adorn the floor through the hall. The kitchen counters are covered with dirty plates and packets of food. Jamie looks into a bedroom on the right as he passes; the bed is swamped in clothes. The whole place is dark.

The destruction continues in the lounge. Stepping in, Jamie stands in the centre looking around. Clothes, towels and bedding are piled against the walls. Light seeps from a lamp buried in one corner. There's almost no furniture. He turns, expecting Isobel to be there. She followed him through the flat, he was sure of it.

She's not. He's alone. The room's empty.

Downstairs a sound system starts up. The music is inaudible, but its rumble passes through the thin floors. Jamie thinks about that person's flat. They've probably got new sofas, matching furniture, fashionable lighting – all on finance, like the cars outside.

There's a noise from the bedroom across the hall.

"It's so nice you've come to see me," comes a voice from the hallway. It's liquid, docile. Isobel.

Jamie sees her appear from the shadows.

"We've got so much to catch up on, so much to do."

She's silhouetted against the warm light of the hallway. Naked.

Chapter 12

"This is, urrm, a friend of ours, Chloe," Emma said as the girl appeared at the door of the kitchen. "Chloe, that's Leo, and this is his *friend*, Allissa."

"Oh, it's good to meet you," Chloe said, not attempting to hide her surprise. Chloe's make up was gratuitously applied and she had squeezed into a dress that seemed far too small.

Chloe looked expectantly from Leo to Allissa to Emma and back again.

"It's a lovely house you have," Allissa said, breaking the silence.

"Thank you," said Emma. "We're pleased with it. Just been in a few months, it's starting to feel like home now."

"Where do you live, Chloe?" Allissa asked, taking a sip of the beer.

"In the next village," Chloe said, before turning to Emma. "Shall we have a glass of prosecco?"

"Being a mum is amazing," Emma said two hours later. They'd moved with their drinks to the large front room. "I don't think I've ever felt so proud of anything..." she continued, meticulously cleaning Frankie's orange shit from her hands with a wet wipe for the fourth time since he'd woken up.

"He's got the shits," Andy said, as though no one would have noticed. "Been a nightmare, had it a week."

"Just something he picked up at one of the classes last week," Emma said. "They get everything at this age."

"That's why he shouldn't be going to nursery," Andy said. "Full of grubby kids. Keep him here, I say."

"I, well…" Emma said, her smile unfaltering.

"Do you have any children, Chloe?" Allissa asked.

"No, I'm afraid not. Can't wait though. They're so cute."

Allissa watched Frankie pull a handful of earth from a potted plant. Then while his mum was still preoccupied cleaning herself up, he smeared it across the glass of the patio doors.

"Yeah, he's a top boy. Gunna be just like his dad!" Andy indicated from his slumped position in the armchair. Next to him a table was quickly filling with empty bottles. Draining his current one, he added it to the empties.

"They're not as much work as you think," Andy said, getting up and crossing the room to where Frankie was banging the window. "I don't really know what all the fuss is about."

Picking up the three-year-old, Andy threw him to the ceiling, filling the room with shrieks and laughs.

"Oh my God," Andy said, after the third throw, holding the little boy out in front of him. "Emma, he still fucking stinks. You need to clean him properly."

Allissa watched as Leo sat up a little straighter. He seemed a step away from throwing Andy to the ceiling himself.

"Who wants another beer?" Andy said, looking towards the kitchen door as he crossed the room back to his chair. "You never could keep up, could you Leo?" Andy nodded towards the half-full bottle in Leo's hands.

Chloe giggled nervously and sunk the rest of the prosecco

in her glass.

"Yeah, I'll have one," Allissa said, standing and finishing the half-bottle she had left. "I could drink this weak stuff all day."

Chapter 13

"Finally, we'll get to spend the whole evening together. There's so much I want to do," Isobel says. Jamie tries not to notice the impossible slenderness of her waist and arms, the curve of her hips, the bulge of her breasts. She's approaching in the darkness. Looking so sweet in the half-light.

Jamie's words come slowly. "No, wait, we're, I'm..."

A beautiful woman walking towards him would usually be something good, something he'd strive to engineer. But he knows this won't end well.

"Stop, Isobel. I came... I came here just to talk to you." His words seem aggressive against her tender skin.

"We can talk if you like, baby," her reply is soft and warm. Soft as the light in the room and warm like her skin had been in his hands. "We can do whatever you like."

She's still moving towards him, her hips rolling with each step.

Jamie tries to stay focused. He knows this shouldn't happen. It mustn't happen. It can't happen.

"You just tell me what you want me to do." Liquid words. Each syllable tasting the air with a forked tongue. She's in front of him now. If Jamie were to reach out, he would touch her delicate, naked skin. He knows what that feels like. He sees it in his mind. It would be so easy, right now, and it would feel so good.

He can't.

"No, Isobel," he says, gentler than he intends to. Almost with a laugh. "We are not doing this again."

"I don't know what you're talking about, baby. Undo this," she says, pulling at his belt. Her body presses into his.

"Seriously, Isobel, no," Jamie says, using all the strength he thinks he has. The words sound weak – far too weak. Almost a joke. He feels her body pressing against him. Her hands explore.

Again, Jamie says no, but keeps his hands by his side. He remembers how good she feels.

She kisses his chest and starts to move downwards.

Jamie looks for something to distract him, to pull him from her curse. All he can see is the twist of her body as it intertwines with his. The feel of her soft breath on his skin.

Go. Get out. Now.

Jamie steps backwards. Isobel looks up.

He's moments from something he already knows he'll regret.

"What the fuck do you think you are doing? Get back here now," Isobel says. The soft voice has gone. Her tongue's barbed and bitter.

"No, Isobel, I'm leaving."

"You are not. We are spending the night together. You promised." The word 'promised' is shouted – it reverberates around the room.

As Jamie moves, Isobel blocks the door. One arm on each side.

41

"You need to move out of my way," Jamie says. Isobel doesn't reply. She looks up at him, twisting her face into a snarl and moving her neck to the side. Her eyes glimmer like a threat.

Jamie doesn't see her hand move until he feels a slash across his face. It stings like a whip. Isobel steadies herself for a second attack, nails outstretched to dig into his skin. This time she begins to scream, and the nails fly forwards and back.

Not feeling the lacerations, Jamie pushes past her. He's bigger and the force catches her off balance. Isobel stumbles backwards into the bedroom across the hall.

Jamie doesn't wait. He runs for the door. He's getting out. Getting home. Behind him the screams continue. Blood thumps from his ears to the strike across his cheek.

Out in the hallway. Down the stairs, two at a time.

Leaving the building he passes a neighbour coming back to their flat. Their eyes pause for a moment on his face. He touches his cheek. When he pulls his fingers away there's a streak of red across them.

Red like a warning.

Red like Isobel's hair.

Chapter 14

"How's the business?" Andy asked when they were seated around the table later that evening. In the background a TV sports channel continued to drone on as it had all afternoon.

"Yeah, it's pretty good," Leo said, watching Emma open the cartons of the Indian takeaway which had just arrived. "Been keeping really busy. A new case up in Scotland at the moment and a few smaller bits and bobs."

"You got really lucky with all that media exposure," Andy said. "When I started my business, I didn't have anything like that. Had to do it through hard work alone. And I'm doing alright being able to provide a home like this for my family."

"Yes, you are," Leo smiled. *With the help of my parents paying most of the deposit and Emma's well-paid job in marketing.*

"How are things at the moment?" Leo asked.

"Really, yeah, really good. Never better." Andy turned to face Emma who had finally sat down. "In fact, we don't think you should go back to work, do we babe?"

"Well, we've not really decided. I like work. I worked hard for that job."

"Yeah but you're a mum now. Frankie is the most important thing. A child of mine needs to be the number one priority."

43

Emma, who had just put Frankie to bed after the whole day of feeding, changing and stopping him from doing dangerous things, looked exhausted.

"Get us another lot of drinks, babe," Andy said as Emma took her first bite of the meal. "You still in the bedsit?" he directed towards Leo.

"Yeah for now. The *flat...*" Leo emphasised the word, "does the job now while work is so busy. When the business is more established, we may look for something else."

"It's a nice flat," Allissa said.

"I've got a mate that's an estate agent round here. He's got a few places on the market you might like. I told him you were half-looking to make a move this way."

"Then you could really take a part in Frankie's life," Emma added, putting her knife and fork down and getting to her feet. "Do you need another drink, Chloe?"

Across the table from Leo, Chloe answered with a long slurp of the vodka and coke. She had quietened down after the third or fourth drink. Leo calculated she must now be approaching double figures. Catching Leo's eye across the table she crunched a poppadum into her mouth, spraying crumbs across her exposed cleavage.

"I'm alright," Leo said finally, looking at Allissa. "I like it in Brighton and if I move anywhere, I'll sort it myself. Thanks though."

"Alright," Andy said, emptying a carton of chips onto his plate, "just tryna help."

Chapter 15

"What are you doing?" Allissa said, watching Leo remove one of the many blankets from the giant bed in Andy and Emma's spare room.

"Making a bed down here," Leo indicated the space on the floor, "you know... so you can get a good night's sleep up there."

"Don't be an idiot," Allissa said, already beneath the duvet but still fully clothed. "This bed is massive, there's loads of room."

"Are you... are you sure?"

"Yeah, course," Allissa met Leo's stare. "Unless you wanna spend the evening with Chloe. I bet she's got room for you."

"I... well..."

Allissa smiled, enjoying Leo's discomfort.

"There was definitely some animal magnetism there, didn't you think?"

"No, course not. Totally not my type."

"Oh what, you didn't think she was attractive? All those curves?" Allissa held her hands in front of her chest in mockery of Chloe's figure.

Leo, realizing he was now staring at Allissa's chest, looked away.

"It's not that she's not attractive," he said, busying himself by pulling a bag of toiletries and some tracksuit bottoms from his ruck sack. "It's just, she's not really my... my type." Finding what he needed, Leo crossed the room and opened the door. "I'll go and get ready." With an awkward look back towards Allissa, Leo crossed the hall to the bathroom.

Smiling to herself, Allissa nestled into the bed. It had been an interesting day and now she felt the warm fuzz of multiple beers.

Closing her eyes, Allissa thought about how funny it was that Leo and Emma could grow up together, have almost the same lives and yet be completely different. Then she thought about her own brother and sister. Although they were only half-siblings as Allissa had a different mother, they had turned out very differently too. For a moment she thought about what they would be doing now. Where were they living? She doubted it was in the box room of shabby top floor flat. As sleep started to soften her senses though, Allissa knew she wouldn't change it for anything. And as she heard Leo cross the landing and open the bedroom door, she felt herself smile.

"I'm sorry that was hard work," Leo said in a whisper. He'd changed into his jogging bottoms in the bathroom to negate any awkward undressing in front of Allissa. "They're nice people, but sometimes I don't know what..." Seeing Allissa snuggled beneath the duvet, he stopped talking. Watching the gentle rise and fall of the covers with just a tuft of Allissa's hair visible, Leo found himself smiling. Silently, he put the bag of toiletries down, folded his jeans, lifted the duvet and slid into the bed.

Sharing his flat with Allissa for the last few months, Leo had got used to spending time with her. He'd come to expect her late rises and monosyllabic morning greeting before the first coffee of the day was poured. He knew her routine and had grown fond of seeing her toothbrush in the holder and her clothes on the drying rack in the hall. He had lain awake on more than one occasion and thought of her sleeping in the next room. Just a few feet away, curled up on the bed they'd bought together. But then, as though in penance, he thought of Mya. She was still out there. Still unfound. Still unknown. Sure, the maps and charts had been moved from the wall in the front room to a drawer in his bedroom, but that didn't mean she didn't still occupy his thoughts. He probably didn't think of her every hour, as he had a year ago, but a few times a week she still clawed her way back into his consciousness.

But now, lying next to Alllissa in the big bed, Leo was glad of it. Mya gave him some boundaries. He and Allissa were just colleagues and friends. Close friends, yes, but he was still looking for Mya. Maybe not physically, but emotionally part of him was still looking for the girl with the wide smile and the large eyes.

Switching off the light, Leo lay rigidly on his back, looking up at the ceiling. Friends, that's all they were, that's all they could be.

Chapter 16

L eo woke with what felt like an electric shock. He stared blankly around for a moment until the memories of the previous evening began to seep into his mind. He was at his sister's, in the guest room, with Allissa.

Looking around in the light from the crack beneath the door, he recognised the room and the sleeping figure of Allissa next to him. In a moment of fear, he checked he hadn't rolled across the bed and crossed any invisible lines in the process. All was good. He was fully clothed. On his back. As close to the edge of the bed as possible without falling out.

Feeling the furry mouth of alcohol, Leo reached across for the glass of water he knew he'd left by the side of the bed. That's when he heard it.

Shouting. Raised voices. Indistinct but obvious. Andy and Emma. He couldn't hear what they were arguing about; the words were faint from another part of the house. Raised but also clipped in an attempt to go unnoticed. But to Leo, the anger and resentment was obvious.

Leo lay in the darkness for a few minutes without knowing what to do. Part of him wanted to go down and intervene. If he could hear the voices, then Frankie could too.

The sound of breaking glass made him sit upright in the

bed.

Then the voices went quiet. Angry footsteps.

One set came upstairs while the other stayed down.

Getting out of the bed, checking for the second time he was dressed, Leo crossed the room and opened the bedroom door. Emma stood on the landing. Her face was streaked with tears.

Gone was the relentless composure she had shown all day. Stepping forward, as though operating on instinct, Emma buried her face in Leo's shoulder. At first Leo was taken aback. He hadn't seen Emma like this, ever. Then, realising what he should be doing, Leo closed his arms around her and pulled her in tight.

As Allissa slept, Leo held his sister in the darkness of the landing. For a moment they were children again and he, the older brother, was protecting her from the playground bully. Doing what an older brother should.

Looking over Emma's shoulder, Leo saw light from the kitchen glowing out into the darkened hallway. *What had gone on down there?*

Somewhere in the house Andy moved, then settled. The only sound was Emma's quiet sobbing.

Was this something that happened often? How could anyone treat his sister like this? Leo felt anger start to drum in his chest. His breathing tightened. His arms dropped to his sides.

Letting Emma go, Leo pushed past her and began to descend the stairs. Andy had been a dick for as long as Leo had known him. Sure, he had no idea what Emma saw in him, but you couldn't go around treating people like this. Andy couldn't treat his sister like this.

"Leo, no, leave him," Emma said, still sobbing as Leo reached the middle of the staircase. "He'll be fine in the morning, don't..."

Pausing, Leo looked back up at her. The serene glamour of the woman who had opened the door earlier was gone.

"No," Leo said in a whisper. "He's not treating you like that."

The kitchen looked as it had a few hours earlier. The only difference, the floor was strewn with broken glass.

"It was an accident," Emma said, walking up behind him. "I shouldn't have wound him up when he had been drinking. I know what he gets like."

"This is not your fault. This is in no way your fault," Leo said, turning and holding her by the shoulders.

Crossing the hallway, Leo pushed open the lounge door. The lights were on and the insipid smell of stale beer hung over the room. Andy sat in his armchair snoring loudly. His head lolled forwards and a pool of dribble collected on his shirt.

"Leave him, don't wake him up now. He'll be fine in the morning. It'll all be fine in the morning."

Saying the words brought a fresh wave of sobs to Emma's fragile body.

Leo considered the sleeping man. He was out of it. Nothing would wake him now. Even if they did, what use was a conversation with an angry drunk?

"Fine," Leo said, "but we need to talk about this."

Emma nodded, Leo put his arm around her and led her back to the kitchen. While Emma sat at the dining table, Leo filled and clicked on the kettle. While it rumbled to the boil, he swept up the broken glass and put it in the bin.

When he and Emma were sat with steaming mugs of tea, she began to speak.

Chapter 17

On Monday morning Jamie calls the Managing Director to explain everything. It had been weighing on his mind all weekend. He'd thought about making something up, something elaborate and convincing, but had decided the truth was best. He's done nothing to be ashamed of. He just can't see Isobel again.

With only a week of his notice left to serve, he hopes it will be met with understanding. Calling especially early, Jamie hopes that Isobel won't be in yet. He needs to tell his side of the story first.

Tony answers sleepily and Jamie explains. There's a curious silence on the line, like the M.D. is thinking of ways to make it difficult for him.

These MD types can be arseholes. Doesn't matter, I'll be in Hong Kong soon.

Behind him there's a knock at the door. Jamie's still on the phone, but he answers it. It's probably just a parcel. The cold air makes him wince and stings his cheek.

Instinctively, Jamie runs his fingers across the red scratch beneath his left eye.

Two police officers stand in the morning gloom.

"Are you Jamie Price?" the taller one of the two asks.

Jamie nods, and without thinking disconnects his call. His arms drop to his sides.

"We'd like to ask you a few questions about the disappearance of Isobel Clarke."

From his coat, hanging limp in the hall, a strand of red hair falls to the floor.

Chapter 18

When Leo woke, the light of the morning was streaming through the window and Allissa was sitting up next to him. Opening his eyes, he felt as though someone had poured grit beneath his eyelids. He and Emma had stayed up talking for over an hour. She'd said that Andy's moods had deteriorated since Frankie had been born. They now had less money than before, so he wasn't able to do the things he was used to and took that out on her. Emma had promised Leo, convincingly, that Andy had never been violent towards her, despite getting angry. She'd thrown the glass at the wall in her own frustration, then broken down in tears.

Leo had made her promise that she would call someone if she needed help. Call him, call their parents, call a friend. Anyone. Just so long as she wasn't suffering alone.

"You've got tea there," Allissa pointed at the steaming mug on the bed side table, "Emma dropped it in."

Rubbing his eyes, Leo reached for it.

Downstairs, Emma was as cheerful as usual. Having already cleared away the signs of the previous day's food and drink she was about to start making breakfast. Frankie played on the floor, quietly picking up each of his toys and examining it closely.

"Morning," Emma said, as Leo and Allissa came down. "You want coffee, or breakfast, or something?"

"No thanks, it's okay," Leo said. "We need to head off soon, got to get back to Brighton as soon as possible."

Leo and Allissa had agreed to leave early but with the conversation he and Emma had shared the previous night still burning in his mind, Leo felt unsure.

"Yeah, sorry," Allissa said, "we've got a mad week ahead and sorting through some things this afternoon will make it all so much easier."

"Sure, yes, no problem," Emma nodded, busying herself with the dishwasher. Leo felt a pang of guilt as he noticed a dozen eggs and a packet of bacon on the counter.

"We'll stay if you've prepared something…"

"No, honestly, it's all good," Emma said, clanging a pan into a drawer.

"I'll go and check we've got everything," Allissa said, turning back towards the stairs.

"Stop for a moment." Leo took a stack of bowls from Emma's hands. "Are you ok?"

"Of course, why wouldn't I be?"

"It was just, last night. I'm really worried about you."

There was so much more he wanted to say – *come with us now* – *you deserve so much better* – *let's get you away from here* – but he just couldn't. In many ways this was the life Emma had always wanted, the house, the baby, the husband – even if cracks were forming beneath the wallpaper.

"He was just drunk, we both were. He's under a lot of stress at the moment. It's nothing."

"It didn't sound like nothing."

54

"Look, he had a lot to drink. He'll be up soon, and it'll be forgotten. It always is."

"He doesn't know how lucky he is," Leo said looking around the kitchen, trying not to be concerned about it *always* being forgotten.

On the floor, Frankie dropped the toy he was examining and crawled over to the plant in the corner. Reaching behind the large pot, he pulled up something that had lain hidden and studied it carefully.

"You deserve so much better," Leo said, before he really knew what he was saying.

"He's my husband," Emma replied sharply. "He *is* a good man."

"Make sure he is, because you and that little boy deserve it," Leo said looking towards Frankie. Frankie, who was about to put a long, glinting shard of glass in his mouth.

Chapter 19

"Just explain, in your own words, what happened," asks one of the police officers across the table from Jamie. He can't be any older than Jamie himself. On the table next to them a recording system hums. A reminder that they're not in private.

"Where do you want me to start?" Jamie asks. He's being helpful, just helping the police with their enquiries.

"When did you first get to know Isobel in a non-professional capacity?" the other officer says. He's older and looks as though his years in the force have drained the colour from his face. He is the same monochromatic hue as the interview room they're in.

Jamie clears his throat and begins. The night of the staff party, the balcony, the drinks, the hotel. The conversation in the office the following morning. The younger officer sits back. He looks relaxed, his posture suggests understanding.

There's a knock at the door. It opens.

"You'll want to see this, Gov."

"Excuse us for a moment." Both officers stand and leave the room.

Just helping the police with their enquiries. Nothing to worry about, it'll all be cleared up soon.

56

Sitting alone, Jamie finds himself staring into the single black eye of the camera on the wall, the only feature in the grey room.

A room without windows. He'll become used to that.

"I'm afraid," says the younger police officer, taking his seat again, "that what we've just learned changes things a little. I do wish you'd told us this."

"What?"

"Just to remind you it is within your rights to have legal counsel. If you don't have a solicitor, we can arrange one for you."

"What? I'm just here to help you, I'm not under arrest, am I?"

"No."

"Not yet," adds the older officer.

"We've just learned from your employer that Isobel made a complaint about you." The officer pulls a piece of paper from a file and lays it on the desk. "Almost a month ago. I'll read part of it now. 'He just keeps following me and trying to talk to me, it's really unsettling. I've said no. I've told him I don't want anything to do with him, but he just won't listen. He's asked for my number three times. I've blocked him on social media. I don't want to cause trouble, but I want him to leave me alone and don't know what else to do.'"

Four eyes bore into Jamie. The grey-haired officer leans forward and extends a chubby finger.

"She's a good-looking girl." He pulls a colour photograph from the file. "Beautiful actually. And you're expecting us to believe that she's been chasing you?"

Jamie doesn't reply. The grinding gears of the machine record his silence, and the single black eye of the camera watches unfaltering.

Isobel is out there somewhere, he knows that, but from inside this grey room there's nothing he can do.

"I think I need that solicitor," Jamie says in a quivering voice.

"I think you probably do. Interview terminated."

Chapter 20

Pulling away from the kerb in the BMW, Leo couldn't get the image of Frankie and the glass from his mind. His small hand curved around the razor-sharp edges. His wide-eyed interest as it glimmered in the light. Leo had been the first across the kitchen and taken the glass from him while Emma held him still.

"She's going to have to be careful," Allissa said as Leo turned on to the main road.

"What's that?"

"That Andy isn't a nice bloke. What you said about him before was right, I wouldn't trust him at all."

"Yeah, there's something not right there." Leo thought about the late-night conversation.

"I hate blokes like that," Allissa said, looking out of the window. "Just because they've got a dick, they think they can treat women badly. It really winds me up."

"Yeah, I don't like leaving her there," Leo said, "but she wouldn't come with us."

"What, you asked her?"

"Yeah, we spoke last night for ages," Leo said, detailing the late-night conversation he and Emma had shared. When he'd finished, Allissa stared silently out of the window.

"We're going to have to come down here more often then," she said, turning to Leo. "They're family and they need you."

Leo knew Allissa was right. Although disaster had been averted this time, the image of Frankie and the shard of glass would live with him long after their journey home. Before leaving he had made Emma promise again that she would call if she needed him.

"Get these jobs done this week," Leo said, thinking out loud, "and I'll arrange something. We could even come and work over here for a few days."

Allissa nodded in agreement.

"Hey, that girl last night was funny though," she said, her tone of voice lightening.

"I know, I thought that too."

"Sorry, didn't mean to get in the way of true love," Allissa said wryly.

"Yeah, she's totally my type."

As Allissa nestled into the seat and shut her eyes, Leo thought of the girls he had introduced Emma to over the years. None were like Chloe. There was one whilst he was at uni, then a couple in the following years. All were nice, but for some reason things didn't happen.

Then there was Mya. She'd been different in every way. She was confident, bold, happy – and for a time she made Leo feel the same. She took away his anxieties and frustrations. At first Emma had liked her too. But that soon changed after Mya disappeared. When she stopped being Leo's girlfriend and became his first missing person. Now she was just a fleeting thought, a stroke of springtime sunshine, warming the ground briefly before disappearing again into a swirl of grey.

Merging onto the motorway, Leo pushed the car a little

harder. Beside him, Allissa slept. Again, the image of Frankie and the glass swam into his mind.

Thinking of the promise he'd made to Emma; Leo knew he would always be there for her. He also knew in the next few months he would have to make more of an effort. He just hoped that she would call before anything happened that wouldn't be alright in the morning.

Chapter 21

"We're going to need to be honest with each other," the lawyer says. He's someone Jamie's brother knows but already Jamie's not sure. Unbuttoning his jacket, he slides his briefcase onto the desk.

"Yes, of course, I just need this to be sorted out." Jamie's lost count of the number of hours he's been in this room now.

"Well it looks to me, Jamie, can I call you Jamie? Is that okay?" The lawyer continues without waiting, "I'm Daniel by the way, Daniel Cottesmore." He takes a business card from his pocket and passes it across to Jamie.

Yeah, as if I can call anyone.

"It looks to me like we've got a tricky situation here. What have you told them already?"

"Just the truth, that I was there, then I left and have no idea where she is now."

"Yes, yes. I see." He removes a folder from the briefcase and opens it. "Well that stands up. But what about this complaint at work?"

"It's the first I've heard of it. It's made up. Rubbish."

"Right, yes, of course. But we will need more than that. How do you explain her hair fibres on your coat?"

"Well, I was there. I'm not denying that."

"Of course, of course."

"And the scratch?" the lawyer points towards Jamie's face.

"She hit me. The girl's mental."

"Well, we can't prove she's mental. In fact, looking at the profile here she seems pretty normal."

The lawyer looks at Jamie. His eyes are dark. Jamie doesn't reply.

"It's my job to ask these difficult questions. They're better coming from me than the police. I'm on your side."

There's a knock at the door, and the lawyer gets up to answer it. One of the officers hands him another file. Sitting back down, the lawyer opens it.

"In the boot of your car," the lawyer says, inhaling.

"What?"

"They've found traces of her blood in the boot of your car. They're charging you with murder."

Chapter 22

Brighton was wrapped up in springtime when Allissa woke up. Through the window of the car, the wide, steep, tree-lined streets looked warm. Small shoots of the coming spring were starting to appear on the gnarled limbs of the Victorian beeches – hinting that there was yet life beneath the desiccated bark.

Passing a group of university students, Allissa thought about what she was like at that age. Wrapped up in her ambition to change the world, to make a difference. Her family had wanted her to go into law, but she couldn't be part of that.

She wondered, watching the group make their way down the steep street, what she would have thought of her life now. One thing was certain, there was no way she could have predicted she would be running a missing persons' agency. But she had to admit that it did bring her happiness. It was exhilarating to help find lost people. To reunite families and friends.

Parking the car as close to the flat as possible, Leo got out and fed the meter enough money to last until the following morning. Allissa had enjoyed them having a car – it was a shame it would be going back. Maybe if business went well, they could get one of their own.

"I'll take the bags," Leo said, slinging them both across his shoulders.

"Fine," Allissa nodded, smiling. If he wanted to prove his masculinity by carrying two small bags up a flight of stairs, she wasn't going to argue.

Unlocking the door of the flat as Leo laboured up behind her, Allissa looked around at the apartment. The worn-out carpets, discoloured walls and every available surface covered with papers, maps and books, made her feel at home. It was the first time she'd felt that way in over two years. Of course, she'd found something of a home in Kathmandu. She'd set up a guesthouse there to give vulnerable women a place to stay and work. It had become their home and helped get their lives back together. But Allissa had just provided the money to set the place up, she was not one of the girls. She didn't feel the sense of belonging they did.

Years ago, the house in Berkshire in which she'd lived with her family had been home. But finding out what her dad had done had shattered that feeling.

Now in the simple, small and untidy flat her and Leo shared in the roof space of a Victorian house, Allissa felt an unusual warmth.

Wondering how much that was to do with her father now being in jail, Allissa picked up the letters which had dropped through the door. No one was looking for her now, no one would be waiting for her. The phone could ring, or the doorbell could go without her needing to worry. It felt good.

Stepping into the kitchen, Allissa flicked through the letters. Although their address wasn't on the website, court orders and other legal information needed to be applied for in old-fashioned pen and ink. As such they usually received a few letters a week which Allissa had taken upon herself to sort.

The room wobbled as Allissa glanced at the second letter in the stack. She felt her breath become short. In her mind she was back there, hiding behind the door, listening to her step-mum accuse her dad of the most horrible things.

Leaning back on the counter to steady herself, she turned the letter over. It couldn't be, could it?

Chapter 23

"Help, help, there's a man outside my flat. He's trying to get in. It's a guy I work with, Jamie Price." Isobel's voice plays from a laptop. Jamie and the lawyer sit opposite the two detectives. The younger one watches the screen of the computer, the older stares at Jamie.

There's a pause on the recording and a crack in the background. Inaudible shouting follows.

"He's outside trying to get in, he's kicking the door..." The emotionless tone of the operator asks a question before Isobel's voice pours out once more. "Get here quickly... please... please..."

The younger detective presses a key and the voice disappears.

"What time did you say you went to see Miss Clarke?" the older officer asks, leaning across the table.

"Mr Price has nothing to say."

"We know you were there and now this comes to light. She didn't even get a chance to say her address. But we tracked it to the block of flats. So, what time did you get there?"

Jamie stutters before the lawyer interrupts.

"Don't say anything at this time."

"Just tell us what you did, then we can start to talk properly."

Jamie looks from one detective to the other. Both wear hard, unforgiving stares.

"I need to talk with my client now," the lawyer says.

With a grumble, the detectives leave the room, closing the door behind them. The lawyer stands and begins to pace.

"It's not looking good. We really need something here, Jamie."

"What we need to do is find Isobel," Jamie says, watching him step back and forth. The lawyer rubs his chin in thought. "Find Isobel. She's got to be somewhere," Jamie says again.

"It'll cost you. Investigators aren't cheap."

"It'll be worth it to find her."

"But you're right, she's got to be somewhere." The lawyer crosses back to the table, unsnaps his briefcase, packs his papers and slides into his jacket. "I think I know someone who will be able to help," he says crossing to the door. "I'll find the address for you, but the rest is up to you."

"Fine," Jamie says as the door is opened from the outside. "We just need to find her."

Again, Jamie is alone in the grey room, just the camera's unblinking stare for company.

Chapter 24

It was a bright spring day beneath a sky of unforgiving blue as Leo walked towards HMP Wandsworth. The prison crouched in a south London suburb of expensive houses and fast cars, as though lost amid a game of Dickensian hide and seek.

Walking beneath the prison's soot-darkened turrets, Leo felt a shudder, even though he wouldn't be staying long.

He had been asked to visit the prison two days before in an unexpected letter. At first Allissa feared it was from her father, Blake Stockwell, who was also making use of the prison's hospitality. It wasn't. The sender was someone neither Leo nor Allissa had ever heard of. A man named Jamie Price, whose communication made clear he was in trouble and needed help.

The case had been instantly interesting to Leo. It wasn't a case of the classic missing person. There was something more to it, and before he'd finished reading it out loud in the kitchen, he'd decided he would visit Jamie Price in person.

Inside the visitors' entrance, Leo was shown into a small room to sign in and have his ID scanned. Two people sat waiting in sagging chairs. A pale, tired-looking woman held a tiny baby as it slept.

Two guards sat behind a small desk; one entered Leo's information on a computer without breaking their conversation.

"I got a taxi home from town at the weekend," the guard on the right said, "and the driver was an absolute charlatan. Charged me fifty quid – he should be in 'ere."

Leo found himself smiling. To him, coming to a place like this was an uncomfortable, alien experience. To these guys it was normal. Just another day.

"Look into that camera," the guard on the left said. Leo forced a smile.

"It was a twenny minute drive, no more than a fiver in petrol…"

"Very nice," The visitor's badge was torn from the printer and handed to Leo. "You're a natural. Keep this on ya. Go press the buzzer on that door."

The door buzzed and was opened by another guard in a bright white shirt. Leo followed him through grey corridors, deep into the prison. Looking around as they walked, Leo felt the building closing in around him. Shallowing him. Crushing him into nothing. Forcing him into a place of no escape. Feeling his chest tighten as his anxiety rose, Leo concentrated on his footsteps.

Breathe in for two. Out for two. In for two. Out for two.

"You've got ten minutes," the guard said, stopping outside a grey metal door.

Leo forced another deep breath. He was glad it was only ten minutes.

"I'll be just outside," the guard said, grinding a key in the lock and pushing the door open.

Leo swallowed, nodded and stepped inside.

Jamie Price was in his mid-thirties, Leo assumed. He was

fresh-faced and attractive. He had the look of someone who, outside of the prison's walls, took pride in their appearance. Now, dark rings encircled his eyes and the grey prison clothes gave the look of someone crumbling away from the inside out.

"Leo, thanks for coming," Jamie said, reaching over to shake Leo's hand. The room was uncomfortable, small, windowless. The air was thick and tasted of disinfectant. Leo nodded and took a deep breath. Ten minutes. He could do that.

"I need to get straight to it, we don't have a lot of time," Jamie said. Leo took the seat opposite him and pulled a note pad and pen from his bag. Without delay, Jamie talked through the night he had spent with Isobel, her subsequent disappearance and his arrest. Leo took notes and asked Jamie to repeat some details just to make sure he had things correct.

"I'll give you the number of my lawyer," Jamie said. "He's a bit of a dick, but he will give you what you need."

"So far," Leo said, "I get what's happened to you, but I don't see how I can help you. I search for missing people, I'm not a lawyer."

"I did not kill Isobel Clarke," Jamie said, his hands balling into fists on the table.

"Right, but –"

"She has to be somewhere. Someone can't just disappear. Maybe she's in this country using a false identity, or maybe she's fled abroad."

Leo nodded. He knew it was rarely that simple. The hard truth of it was that people could just disappear. They did with alarming frequency.

"She's a clever woman. She must have some kind of plan."

"Sure, but why?" Leo asked, "If she wanted to run away, she

could. Why does she want you locked up?"

"Revenge maybe?" Jamie offered.

"But at some point," Leo said, "she's going to need to come out of hiding and you'll be released and she'll be charged. What she's done is illegal. Surely she'd realize that?"

Jamie shrugged.

"You're right, there must be more to it than revenge. But I'm not sure what."

Leo tapped the nib of his pen on the paper and looked around the room. Feeling the grey walls begin to suffocate him, he turned his focus to Jamie.

"Tell me about the job you were supposed to be starting," Leo asked, and after a pause, "if that's alright. The more I know, the more I'll be able to help."

"Sure, fine. It was basically my dream job. Working for a firm of architects in Hong Kong. They design high rise buildings all across Asia. I'd been working for years to get the right experience to do that. There's only a handful of companies like them in the world."

"What's the company called?"

"OZ Architecture."

Leo made a note of it; he was on to the third page of his notepad.

"Two minutes," the guard shouted from outside.

"What job did Isobel do?"

"She worked in the interiors department."

Leo nodded.

"When did you get the job in Hong Kong?"

"About six months ago."

"Okay, was it through an agency or something, or did you go straight there?"

"No, an agency sorted it all. They place people all over the world in construction."

Leo made a note of that too.

"Okay, let me look into it for you. I'm going to need a few things from you though. A copy of your latest bank statements to check there's nothing suspicious there. That'll rule out any financial motivations Isobel might have. A recent photo and a copy of your ID. And the down payment to pay our expenses."

"Sure, contact my brother he will sort all of those things for you."

Behind Leo, the door clattered open.

"Thank you for coming," Jamie said reaching out and touching Leo on the back of the hand. "Believe me, I haven't done anything. I'm innocent. You find Isobel and I can have my life back."

"Out now," the guard said, putting his hand on Leo's shoulder.

"I'll look into it," Leo said as he was led out of the room and back into the warren of grey corridors.

Chapter 25

The final tourists of the day shuffle up to the Victoria Peak viewing platform. Behind them, Hong Kong stretches back into golden twilight as though posing just for their photos. The lights of the buildings clustered around the slope begin to flicker to life. Each building strains to reach upwards, although none are as high as The Peak itself.

In the middle's a girl with red hair tied high on her head. She's pretty. She's talking to the people around her as though they've known each other for months when, in reality, it's been minutes.

Behind her, the silver slither of Kowloon Bay is flecked with the Star Ferries, junk boats and floating restaurants which cruise between Hong Kong island and Kowloon.

As the sun descends behind the final wisps of cloud, a cruise ship – a wall of white against the grey-blue channel – sounds its horn as it breaks from the land.

The group smiles for pictures. Gazing into lenses, they think of likes, digital thumbs up and jealous friends.

Isobel doesn't; she's long since forgotten social media, she doesn't care about that. That's one compromise with pretending to be dead. But there's no one she wants to talk to anyway. She's here, and that's all that matters now.

Behind her, Kowloon stretches into nothing. Neon lights will soon flicker into a chaos of multi-coloured promises. The smells of fish sauce and stir-fried onions will tumble into the street and a new kind of day will begin. The man-made day which cities like this are dragged through every time the sun goes down.

Beyond Kowloon, mainland China lurks. A monolithic landmass stretching almost halfway back to London. A place to which Isobel has no want to return.

The phone call was a stroke of genius and it was so easy to do. Just a few shouts down the phone with some recorded noise playing in the background. She just needed something, something to guarantee he'd be charged. To guarantee they wouldn't come looking for her.

Watching the glimmering buildings against the angry sky, Isobel unclips her hair and lets it fall over her shoulders.

The journey to Hong Kong wasn't easy. First overland from London to Paris on the coach. She knew passport checks on leaving the UK to Europe on coaches were random, and she was lucky to avoid it. Then more busses and trains, arriving in Istanbul three days later. From there, a flight to Hong Kong. Her hope was that if anyone was looking for her, they wouldn't think to check flights from that far away. So far, it's seemed to work. There's been no knock at the door, no dark figures waiting for her – no one seems to be interested at all.

But it's tomorrow when the real fun will begin. The job she's always wanted. The job she deserves. The only issue remains. She must become Jamie Price.

Chapter 26

The first few days of an investigation were always the hardest, Leo thought as he and Allissa sat around their coffee table, piled high with maps and notes from the Edinburgh case. The start was hard because not only did they know nothing, but they didn't know what they were looking for. As such, everything had to be kept and logged, in case, at some point soon, its relevance became clear.

"This could be an interesting one," Leo said, explaining what Jamie had told him. Leo knew if it went well it also had the potential to become a high-profile case.

"But is there actually anything to suggest he's telling the truth?"

"I suppose not. There's nothing concrete, but I feel like he's telling the truth. It would be pointless to hire someone to investigate if you thought what they might find would incriminate you further."

"Alright," nodded Allissa. "Where do we start?"

"I'm going to call the brother, get anything I can from him sent over. Bank statements, ID, login to his social media if possible. We need to gather everything we can about both people involved. Jamie and Isobel. Who they are, where they're from, what they do. Get to know them. Then we'll see if anything jumps out at us."

"Sure." Allissa reached for the laptop as Leo started to clear the coffee table. The maps of Edinburgh would have to go away. Leo had almost finished passing it on to his local contact anyway. Now they needed space to think about this new case. To draw things together and make connections. Anything that would give them a clue where Isobel, if she was alive, would have gone.

Chapter 27

"Hi," Isobel mouthed silently to the receptionist who was speaking quickly into her headset. Behind the reception desk the open plan office of OZ Architecture occupied the entire floor. Through the full height windows, the outlines of the surrounding towers of Hong Kong Island glimmered in the bright morning.

Despite the size of the office, no more than a dozen people seemed to be working. Isobel tried to swallow her nerves. She had imagined the company employing four times that. She thought it would be a company so big she could join the team and work unnoticed.

"Hello, can I help you?" the receptionist said, switching to English from the telephone conversation she'd just ended.

"I'm Jamie Price," Isobel said, patting down her skirt and straightening the shirt which she knew hinted at her curves beneath. "I start work here today."

"Welcome," smiled the young lady, microphone and earpiece dangling from her head. "Take a seat and I'll let the director know you're here. He likes to welcome new staff personally."

"Okay, thanks," Isobel said, swallowing hard. Today was risky. There was a chance she would be found out instantly. But she needed this so much. She deserved it. This was the only way. It had to be worth the risk.

Before leaving, Isobel had done her research. Jamie had been interviewed and recommended for the position by an agency in the UK. She knew he hadn't visited the company in Hong Kong, but his details would have been passed on by the agent. What she was counting on, what she was betting her life on, was that they hadn't received a photograph. Or if they had, it wouldn't be remembered.

She hadn't expected the team to be only twelve people and to be meeting the director on her first day.

Sitting on a minimalist plastic moulded chair, Isobel crossed and re-crossed her legs. She already had her excuse prepared if he noticed. She'd look confused, make some noise about there being a mix up at the agency. Would they believe that the agency had got the details wrong without checking? It was possible.

Opening her bag, Isobel gripped the passport she'd had forged before leaving the UK. The fake was good, it looked and felt just like her own passport stashed back in her hotel. This one had previously belonged to someone from Essex. They'd used it well. Isobel had been through it at least ten times and made sure she could say a few words about each of the places she was supposed to have visited.

Of course, Cambodia. I spent a week at Angkor Wat, incredible place.

The previous owner's address was still printed in it, now beneath her picture. She'd already used it to set up a bank account for her wages to be paid into.

Although the fake was good, she'd been warned it wouldn't pass an electronic scan. As such, she'd used her own passport on the flight from Istanbul to Hong Kong. It hadn't seemed to raise any alarms. Maybe no one was even looking for Isobel Clarke.

"Jamie," came a male voice.

Isobel shut the passport and pushed it back into the bag.

"Yes," she stood, holding the bag awkwardly in front of her for a moment before letting it drop to her side.

"I'm Sam Yee," said the man crossing the office towards the reception area. Isobel noticed his eyes drift across her figure before meeting hers.

"Jamie Price," Isobel said, using the name she had practised in the mirror numerous times and taking Yee's hand.

"I trust your journey was fine, and you're settling in well," Yee said. "Come with me, we will have coffee in my office, then you'll meet the team."

Chapter 28

Allissa smiled as she navigated through the first few pages of her search. Beside her, Leo cleared the coffee table of their previous case's notes and files. Having a clean slate to start with was one of their favourite parts of the job. They'd start with nothing and build up a working knowledge of a person or people until they knew them like friends. Although Allissa had never been trained in psychology, she enjoyed making assumptions about people she'd never met. So far, most of her assumptions had turned out to be close to the truth.

As Leo dropped the piled-up papers from the Edinburgh case into a large plastic box and slid them beneath the table, Allissa scrolled through the search results for "Jamie Price Architect."

"That's interesting," she said looking down the results.

"What?"

"None of these results are about our Jamie Price. You'd expect someone like that to have a LinkedIn account or something, especially if he was looking for work."

Leo agreed, dropping to the sofa next to Allissa.

"Jamie Price is a common name. There are a few of him, but you'd expect him to have been in the top couple of pages."

Allissa clicked through to the next page of results.

"You're right. He wasn't a shy or introverted type of guy. He definitely would have used social media," Leo said leaning in to better see the screen. Then, feeling Allissa's arm brush his, he shuffled awkwardly away.

"Particularly if he was planning to work abroad. It would then become especially important to keep in touch with friends and family," Allissa said.

"Yes, let me check with his brother. I'll get him to send over the links to the accounts he knows about. Want a drink?"

Allissa nodded as Leo crossed the room, picked up his phone from the desk and walked into the kitchen. Allissa could hear him fill the kettle and then switch it on.

"Yes, he definitely has Facebook, LinkedIn and Instagram," Leo said, coming back into the room a few minutes later with two cups of coffee. "His brother is going to look them up and send us over the links now. He's also going to make the down payment and send us the other bits we need to really get started."

"Okay, cool, maybe they just weren't coming up for some reason. I think I've found a picture of Isobel Clarke though, based on the description." Allissa turned the screen to show Leo the picture of a slim red-haired woman in a revealing dress. "Pretty girl, isn't she?" Allissa watched Leo examine the picture.

"I suppose so," Leo said dismissively as his phone rung in his hand. "It's Jamie's brother again," he said answering. "What… Right… No that shouldn't have happened… that's really interesting, thanks… okay…"

"So that's interesting," Leo said, ending the call and looking at Allissa. "For some reason all of Jamie's social media accounts have been deactivated."

"Could he have done that?"

"He wouldn't have had a chance to do that himself, and he hadn't asked his brother to."

"Very strange," Allissa said frowning. This case was starting to get interesting.

Chapter 29

"Come in, sit down," Yee said, holding the door of his office open. Walking past him, Isobel noticed his eyes sink across her figure.

"This is one of my favourite parts of the job," Yee said, indicating the leather chairs in the corner, beside the wall of glass. Finishing their wander, his eyes met Isobel's. "Welcoming new members of the team, I mean, it's so exciting. I love it."

Isobel paused to look out of the window. Although the view from the main office was impressive, from here it was better. The buildings outside lined up in a tonal tapestry of glass around a golden strip of shimmering sea.

"Yes, it's a beautiful view isn't it?" Yee said.

"It is beautiful," Isobel repeated, pulling herself away from the view. Checking her skirt was in place she lowered herself into the chair opposite Yee.

Yee undid his dark jacket and leaned back into the chair, folding his arms. The rising sleeve exposed a gold watch on his left wrist.

"Coffee?" Yee asked, the leather creaking as he shifted in his seat.

Isobel nodded. Yee removed his phone and pressed a few buttons.

"You have a lovely office," Isobel said, looking around. Dark wood contrasted the light streaming through the windows and white walls were adorned with bright modern art.

"Thank you, we designed this building," Yee said extending an arm. "It was the first time we'd designed anything on Hong Kong Island. At the time, we couldn't afford to have a place here. A few years later though, when things were going well, this top floor became available. I had to take it. It was a sign." Yee's voice was high-pitched, sibilant and hinted at an expensive education.

"Do you believe in signs, Jamie?" Yee asked, leaning back into the chair again, his arms folded tightly.

"How do you mean?"

"Do you believe that the universe gives us signs to tell us something is right?"

Isobel thought for a moment.

"Yes, I suppose I do," she said. "Although you have to work for these things too," she added.

"Yes, of course, you're quite right. But it has seemed to me that if you focus on something enough," Yee said, fixing Isobel with a stare. "If you want it enough, somehow it'll happen."

"I suppose so," Isobel said. "I'm very ambitious if that's what you mean. When I know I want something, I work towards it for years if I need to, like this job." Isobel straightened her back as she spoke.

"Yes, of course." Yee spun his phone between thumb and finger.

The door opened and the receptionist entered with two cups on a tray. Placing them on the small table between the pair, she retreated again.

"You have to drink it when it's hot." Yee reached across,

picked up one of the cups and sipped from it flamboyantly.

Isobel watched as he drained the steaming cup, then placed it back on the table.

"We're all very intimate here," Yee said, looking directly at Isobel. She wasn't sure what he meant. "We're a small team. I hand-pick the people I want to work with, a very *intimate* group of people."

"Yes, I'm looking forward to meeting everyone," Isobel said, smiling and reaching for the coffee.

"You'll fit right in." Yee looked through the window beyond Isobel. "Tell me," he said, focusing on Isobel again. "What do you think is your biggest success so far?"

Isobel talked about one of the projects she'd worked on last year. A new office block in Hounslow. She tried to keep as close to the truth as possible in case he looked it up. Only her personal involvement was exaggerated.

"What about outside of work?" Yee asked, his gaze unfaltering.

Isobel felt a prickle of sweat on her forehead as she thought. She'd run a half marathon two years before. Yee nodded impressively as she told him.

"Tell me, Jamie. What do you make of that picture, the large one in the centre?" Without taking his eyes off Isobel, Yee pointed to the wall behind him. The painting was colourful. Shapes of blue, black and green danced in what seemed like chaotic and senseless circles across an orange background.

"I've never..." Isobel started, before pausing. Yee turned briefly to look at the painting. When he turned back, he was grinning.

It's a sign, Isobel thought, *he's looking for a sign*. Saying she didn't really get modern art definitely wouldn't wash.

"Hmm," she said bristling, arching her shoulders and squinting at the canvas. Yee's eyes didn't leave her. "It's interesting, I've not seen it before."

"Yes, it's one of my favourites. What do you think it's about?"

Isobel inhaled slowly; it was as though the office had got hotter.

"It... Well it looks, to me at least, like there's some kind of pain there." She lifted an arm as though pointing something out. "Like the artist is trying to escape something, you know? I think I'd have to know more about it to make a proper judgement."

"Interesting," Yee hissed.

"It's great, I like it," Isobel added in case the director was going to say he had painted it himself.

Yee looked at her unblinking.

"Good, me too," Yee said, standing. "We'll meet the team now."

"Yes, of course. It is a lovely painting," Isobel said, trying to suppress the shiver she felt as Yee indicated she should walk first.

Chapter 30

Beyond the glass of the bay window, seagulls swooped in the clear springtime air. From inside, through the old windows, their mournful cries were still audible as Leo and Allissa continued with their research.

Leo had to remind himself that this part of an investigation always moved slowly. It took a great effort to get things going; there were always dead ends and wrong turns. Sometimes it would feel like it wasn't worth continuing, like they were stuck, until finally something would click into place. On other occasions the challenge came when information started to be uncovered but didn't fit together yet.

"Any luck?" Leo turned to Allissa who had got up and crossed the room to the printer. A picture of Isobel slid from the humming machine.

"There's almost nothing," Allissa said. "It's very strange. People put all sorts of stuff online, but not this pair. There's hardly a trace. A few pictures where they've appeared with other people, a couple of professional shots, that's it."

Leo nodded. He'd been researching the company Jamie had worked for in London and the one he had planned to work for in Hong Kong. Similarly, nothing interesting stood out to him.

"It makes you think someone has been cleaning up after them, doesn't it?" Allissa said, but Leo was distracted by the receipt of an e-mail.

Silently he read for a minute. It was from Adam Price, Jamie's brother. It contained the documents Leo had requested and confirmation of the down payment. Leo replied in thanks and then set to opening the attachments. The first was a scan of Jamie's passport. In the picture his hair was styled and his jawline bristled with the beginnings of a thin beard. Leo printed it to be added to the evidence on the coffee table.

Next, Leo opened a document which he had asked Adam to put together for him. It amounted to a sort of CV, detailing all the places Jamie had worked or lived, places he'd been and the interests he held. Adam had done a good job. The list was detailed and meticulous, especially considering it had only taken him a couple of hours. Leo sent that to print too.

"There's a lot here," Allissa said, picking it up from the tray.

"I know. But in this case, we're better to have it because getting in touch with Jamie to check something isn't easy." Leo thought of the long grey corridors. He really didn't want to go back there.

Allissa nodded and took the papers over to the coffee table where she arranged them around the picture of Isobel in the middle. Both hoped that soon a pattern or link would appear.

Leo opened the final attachment, Jamie's most recent bank statement. The red and white document filled the screen. At the top his current balance was displayed. Leo nodded, impressed. Jamie was a well-paid guy. Then, wanting to read it chronologically, Leo scrolled back a week. It looked as though all the payments were outgoing, mostly bills and house expenses.

"That's after he was arrested," Allissa said, reading over Leo's shoulder.

Leo scrolled back a further two pages. There, the statement became more densely populated. Jamie seemed to be someone with a busy and affluent social life. Seeing some of the amounts he spent in designer clothes shops and expensive restaurants, Leo exhaled.

"That definitely wasn't a meal for one," Leo said, pointing at one payment for a sumptuous restaurant he'd heard of in central London.

"He paid for a hotel on the same night too," Allissa said.

"That was a week before Isobel made the claim."

"I think we're dealing with a bit of a player here," Allissa said, sinking into a crouch beside Leo.

Continuing to scroll, Leo noticed that, as expected, the number of outgoing payments dropped off shortly before the date of his arrest.

"But that doesn't make sense," Leo said. "Look at the total in the account here," he pointed towards the screen, "it's smaller than the current total at the top of the bill."

"He's been making money while in prison?"

"Well he could have some investments or something, but it's a lot smaller."

"Scroll up, let's see."

"There look," Leo said, pointing out the current total.

"Yeah, so where did that come from?" Allissa said, as the pair began to scan down the document. It didn't take them long to notice the payment that had been made into the account.

"There look," Allissa said again with a gasp, her finger extended towards the screen. Leo smiled. Things had started to fall into place.

Chapter 31

Leaving the offices of OZ Architecture, Isobel felt a sense of calm that she hadn't for a very long time. Sure, she was impersonating someone else. She knew the risks were high, but so were the rewards. And the first day had gone well.

After Yee's awkward introduction to every member of the team, she spent the afternoon going through the systems they used. Some of them she'd seen before, others were new. She had a lot to learn but was confident she could do it.

The best thing – she was no longer dancing to someone else's beat. No longer begging for the recognition she deserved. Isobel was now in control. She was making things happen and that felt good.

Sure, time was limited. She knew someone may come to look for her. But it would probably take them a couple of months and by then she would have proved herself. She could do better than all these men who spent half their time at boozy lunches on the company's money.

In an attempt to buy her as much time as possible, before leaving the UK, Isobel had taken down all of Jamie's social media profiles. The ease involved proved her point about him being undeserving for the role. She had just walked into his office and used his computer while he was out enjoying a long, company-funded lunch. Sure enough, the browser was set to remember the passwords, so all she had to do was change them herself and set the browser to remember the change. Jamie didn't even notice.

Then the night before she disappeared, Isobel logged on at home and disabled the accounts.

As the train rumbled beneath the strip of water separating Hong Kong Island from Kowloon and the rest of mainland China, Isobel smiled. Things were looking up. This was her chance, the chance she'd never had. It was a dream that, with a bit of initiative, was now coming true. She was going to be an architect.

Heading towards the street at Ho Man Tin metro station, Isobel's optimism started to dip with the thought of her grimy hotel. She hadn't minded after her long journey. Now, having seen the elegance of the company's offices and the pictures Yee had showed her of the apartment that would be hers once the finishing touches were applied, the darkening street which she was turning onto seemed unappealing.

On either side of the narrow road, concrete towers blocked out the darkening sky. Night fell more quickly here. The only surviving light was neon glow from the shops and restaurants and the occasional swish of passing cars. This was the problem with doing things unofficially, sometimes you had to take things as they came.

Yee had offered to put her up in a hotel, but hotels required a passport. Isobel couldn't have used her own as the names didn't match, nor could she risk using the fake one for anything non-essential.

So, reluctantly, she'd told the company she would enjoy

spending a few days with friends and had booked into a cheap hotel using her own name.

It wouldn't be for long, she told herself again as she pressed the buzzer on the grimy door.

Without knowing why, Isobel looked left and right down the street. The shadows were thick and within them she thought she could see a vague figure walking towards her. She squinted into the impermeable gloom.

A neon light overhead buzzed to life; its glowing scrawls indecipherable. Looking back down, Isobel saw nothing. The street was empty.

With an involuntary shudder, despite the warmth of the evening, Isobel pulled her jacket tight around her. Now she was seeing things too.

"Shi," came a grizzly voice from the door entry speaker. The man in the reception had given Isobel the creeps yesterday. She shuddered thinking of his bulging eyes moving across her body. She pulled her jacket around her tightly. She didn't want to encourage his leers.

The door clunked as the lock disengaged. Isobel pushed it, and with a final look down the empty street, stepped inside.

Climbing the tight staircase, Isobel again thought of the apartment Yee had showed her. It was part of a new building the company had designed themselves. It looked incredible. From one side the view stretched as far as Hong Kong Island and The Peak and on the other the bustle of Kowloon faded into the glinting ocean.

As Isobel reached the top of the stairs, the buzzer of the hotel's door sounded again. The greasy receptionist picked up the phone amid the noise of the game show on the small TV and barked an answer. Isobel ignored him, glad for his distraction. Pulling the key from her bag, she unlocked the door of her room.

* * *

Why he had been told to follow the girl he didn't know. Sure, she wasn't bad to look at, but this really wasn't his job. Head of Personal Security it said on the door of his office, not some kind of second-rate private detective.

Seeing her turn, he stepped into the doorway of a launderette. The street was darkening by the moment. That was lucky – following people was easier in the dark.

The metro had been a challenge. He had watched her for the entire journey in the reflection of the darkened windows. She hadn't noticed. Of course she hadn't, he was a professional.

Why he had to follow her, he wasn't sure. The boss had just said to keep an eye on her. He was always cautious but didn't normally go to these lengths.

Peering from the doorway, a neon sign above flickering into life, he saw her entering a building up ahead. As she disappeared, he covered the few paces quickly. It was a hotel. The sort of cheap hotel that was really just a few rooms above a shop.

Looking at the windows above, he pressed the buzzer.

A light clicked on in one of the rooms above.

"Shi," came a rough voice from the small speaker.

He exchanged a few words with the voice and the door buzzed again.

Instinctively, he looked left and right before stepping from the dark street into the hotel's dank stairway. He had a deal to make.

Chapter 32

"What does that mean?" Leo said. The numbers he stared at on the screen showed a payment made into Jamie's account from OZ Architecture. That was the company he was supposed to be working for in Hong Kong.

"Well, it could be a mistake, they could have –"

"Paid him even though he's not turned up for work?" Leo interrupted.

"Yeah, it's not likely. Although I wouldn't mind working for them if so."

"I'm really not sure." Leo rubbed his chin. "Let's give them a call and see if they'll tell us anything."

"What time would it be in Hong Kong now?"

Leo pressed a few keys on the computer. "Just after six p.m."

"Someone should be there still." Allissa picked up her phone. "Get the number."

Since he and Allissa had started working together, Leo found himself constantly impressed by how she could get people to open up. Maybe as a result of her time working with vulnerable young women, she had a soft and friendly manner that people seemed to instantly warm to. Leo, on the other hand, seemed to wind people up. He just said what he thought and asked the questions he needed the answers to. A technique which rarely got the answers he wanted.

As such the pair had an unspoken agreement that if there was something to analyse or arrange, that fell to Leo. But if someone needed to be persuaded to give some information, if sensitivity was needed, Allissa was the person for the job.

"Good afternoon," Allissa said when a female voice answered. "I'm looking to get in contact with an employee of yours, Jamie Price."

"What's it concerning?" the voice replied. Allissa thought fast. "I'm from the Tax Office in the UK. It seems your employee is owed a rebate on last year's earnings but we're not sure where to send it."

"What name again?"

"Jamie Price."

There was a silence on the line. In the background one voice called and another answered.

"I'm sorry, I can't pass on personal information," the voice came back.

"I'm not looking for personal information, just to speak with Jamie Price."

"I can't do that. Not in the office."

"Can you at least pass on the message?" Allissa said, pushing for a confirmation. Again, there was a silence, a flurry of typing keys.

"Yes, fine, I'll do it tomorrow. Goodbye," the voice said, before the call was disconnected.

For a moment, Leo and Allissa continued to listen, then they turned to look at each other.

Neither spoke but both minds raced to the same question; how could the receptionist pass on the message if Jamie Price was in a London prison?

"That was some quick thinking." Leo tilted his chair back and knitted his fingers together. "I think we need to go to Hong Kong."

Chapter 33

"It was my birthday yesterday," Leo says to Mya as their boat crosses the ocean of faultless blue from Champon to Kao Tao.

"I knew it was at some point this week," Mya says, without moving. They've been travelling all night on the train from Bangkok. They caught some ragged sleep between midnight and 4am before changing onto a bus to the port. Then, still in darkness, they boarded the boat for the five-hour crossing.

"Did you want me to sing happy birthday to you?"

The top ridge of the sun appears from beneath the lightening ocean.

"No," Leo forces a laugh. "That's okay. Being here is a present, I wasn't expecting anything."

"That's what I thought," Mya says, looking at Leo, sitting next to her, for the first time. Leo notices a glimmer in her eyes. "You must be getting really old now. You'll have to give up soon and go back to wearing those slippers."

"You're catching up," Leo says, putting his arm around her waist and pulling her close. He ignores a resistance in her posture. He doesn't want to think that anything could be wrong.

They've been travelling for nearly two months and home is

beckoning. For the last month, Leo has been carrying an engagement ring in his wallet. He's been waiting for the perfect time, the time when the planets align, when things will just feel right. So far it hasn't appeared.

But time is running out. They're going home soon.

What he doesn't know, what he can't know, is that asking the question will be the easy part. It's what happens later that will be much harder. Because today is the final day they'll spend together. For the next two years it will run through his memory. He will decode and analyse every word and action. Was there a clue? Was there any indication that Mya was planning to go?

Did she know that today would be their last day together? Had she planned all along to slip away under the inky blue of the Kao Tao sky?

He'll find himself clutching at straws for over two years. Two years of searching until he will receive a picture. In that picture Mya will stand, arms outstretched, her smile as wide as ever, her eyes glistening in the private way Leo loved so much, in front of the skyline of Hong Kong.

* * *

It wasn't until the plane circled Hong Kong International Airport that Leo thought about Mya. Once he did, he couldn't stop.

It wasn't that Allissa had replaced Mya at all. They were just friends sharing good times and working together. But Allissa did fill his life with an easy-going contentment he hadn't felt for a long time. In many ways spending time with Allissa was easier than it had ever been with Mya. Mya challenged him.

Their whole trip, the trip she didn't come home from, had been her idea. Leo couldn't imagine Allissa ever doing that. If Leo ever said he didn't want to do something to Allissa, she'd smile, possibly sigh and do it alone. Mya took such reservations as points of conflict and wouldn't stop until Leo submitted to seeing things her way.

Swallowing hard, Leo watched the mottled islands of Hong Kong below as the plane tilted in the thin spring air. They were lining up for landing.

But was Mya still here? Leo knew she had been at some point. There was a picture to prove it. For a moment, Leo wished he knew what Stockwell had known when he'd sent him the photo. The deal had been simple: information on Leo's missing girlfriend for the location of Stockwell's missing daughter. But after what he and Allissa had been through in Kathmandu, Leo knew that wasn't an option. For a fleeting moment, just a heartbeat, he had considered it. He had wanted to see Mya for so long it had felt like a breakthrough. But then, watching Allissa sleeping in the hotel room they'd shared in Pokhara after escaping Stockwell's killers in Kathmandu, Leo knew he couldn't. To do that would be worse than the people who had taken Mya. Or worse than Mya herself if she'd chosen to go. And Stockwell couldn't be trusted anyway.

Mya couldn't still be here, could she?

That picture might have been a year old already by the time he got it. She was probably just visiting for the weekend. She'd be long gone by now. Or maybe, Leo thought as buildings came into view, she was down there somewhere. Somewhere in the city between the glimmering seas.

"Are we nearly there?" Allissa said, waking slowly with the jolts of the manoeuvring plane.

Feeling Allissa move beside him, Leo felt a pang of guilt that he hadn't told her about the picture. There just hadn't been the right time. He hadn't kept it from her on purpose, he hadn't lied to her. They had been through so much at the time he received it that he didn't want to add to her concern. Then when they got home, they were wrapped up in Stockwell's trial and then business picked up.

"Oi, dopey," Allissa said, pulling out one of Leo's earphones. "Is this Hong Kong?"

Leo turned to see Allissa's dozy morning smile.

"Yeah," he said thoughtfully. "We're here."

Chapter 34

"Are you on tomorrow?"

"Yeah, on the afternoon shift."

"Brilliant, well don't stay up too late."

"Just having one or two, see you!" she says, waving to her colleague behind the counter of the coffee shop and stepping out into the early evening.

Pausing for a moment beside the door, she prepares herself for the gauntlet of Nathan Road. The busiest street in Kowloon, even in the evening, it's teeming with shoppers, returning workers and those going out for dinner or drinks. But it's the hawkers, selling everything from cheap gold to expensive drugs, that annoy her. She'd expected that after almost a year of seeing her walk to and from work every day they'd recognise her and stop trying to offer her the same shit. Even a hand in the wrong place can see a salesman try to attach a watch to it, the removal of which is always time-consuming, awkward and fraught with their attempts to sell, sell, sell.

Tying her dark hair high on her head, she pushes her earphones in to drown out the city and attempts a frown. People always say she seems approachable. In this case that's a problem. The smile that's currency all over the world is not good when you need to be quick, get home, get changed and get over to the Island.

Chapter 35

"How far is it?" Allissa asked as they pushed from the metro station and onto the wide pavement of Nathan Road. Despite the darkening evening the street still thronged with people.

"Nathan Mansions, 200 Nathan Road," Leo said, looking from the map on his phone to the surrounding buildings. People jostled past as they spoke.

"This is 150, so just a bit up here. It's not far."

It seemed to Allissa that everything had moved very quickly since Leo had visited Jamie in the prison just ten days ago. Leo had only booked the hotel the day before they left. He'd said it was reasonable considering the location and timescale. Allissa didn't expect much with that introduction, but as long as it had a bed, shower and toilet she'd make do.

As usual, Allissa had dealt with negotiating the money for the job. Leo always seemed to find the process difficult and embarrassing. That meant he would be more likely to settle on a low price just to get the negotiation over with. Allissa didn't care, she was happy to demand whatever they thought was reasonable. If the client didn't accept then that was their loss.

Because this job was going to require travel, she had

demanded ten percent to be paid upfront to cover their costs. The rest would be transferred when they got evidence that led to Jamie's release. Allissa had been comfortable making the demands as she'd seen Jamie's bank accounts and knew he could afford it. His brother didn't argue and transferred what they wanted straight away. The deposit was enough to pay basic expenses but wouldn't put them in a five-star hotel. If they got the evidence though, they would be comfortable for a while. They may even be able to have some time off – if they wanted it.

Walking up the wide pavements, past gleaming displays of jewellery, designer handbags and shoes, Allissa felt slightly dazed by the scale of the city. Maybe it was the broken sleep on the long flight, the time difference or just the different air, but everything seemed loud, colourful and vibrant.

On the side of the building opposite a giant screen showed a video of a supermodel blowing kisses. Distracted by the lights, Allissa felt someone knock her shoulder.

"Sorry, I…" Allissa shouted after the girl. But the girl, with her face down, didn't stop.

Muttering to herself, Allissa rushed to catch up with Leo, who had stopped ahead to look at his phone.

On the opposite side, dwarfed by structures of glass and chrome, stood a discoloured concrete building. The frontage looked green in the humid city and signs in the grimy windows advertised rooms for rent.

"Found it," Leo said, grinning.

As long as it has a bed, toilet and a shower, Allissa thought again, forcing a smile.

The building looked even more decrepit as they crossed the road. Parts of it were covered in mould so thick it looked as though the concrete was bubbling. In places water dripped, discolouring the street where it landed. Signs around the entrance advertised a dozen or so hostels which occupied the building. None seemed to be in any logical order.

"Looks great," Allissa said, stepping past a group of men who smoked and bickered by the door. Inside, Allissa realised the ground floor was used as a small shopping mall. Seeing Leo and Allissa pass, the men at the door stopped their chatter and followed them, shouting the prices of the goods at their stalls.

"You need suit – best suit in Hong Kong."

"Dresses for the lady."

"Shoes and belts, come look, come see, just look."

Allissa waved the men away and followed the signs to the back of the mall where a small crowd gathered around the elevators. Two young Chinese men with greased hair and leather studded jackets joked. A European couple whispered to each other. A Chinese woman carried a basket of yellowed washing under one arm and in the other clasped the hands of two small children as though they were in imminent danger of running away. The children watched Leo and Allissa suspiciously with unblinking stares.

Allissa looked at the children and smiled, their eyes connected with hers. They straightened nervously and pushed themselves behind the wide protective body of their mother. Through the gap beneath her arm they continued to peer at Leo and Allissa.

Allissa waved and one of the children edged forward to get a better view. Then Allissa stuck her tongue out. A smile broke across the face of the larger child. Then Allissa screwed her face up and blew out her cheeks. The children erupted into high pitched laughter. Ignoring the children's noise, their mother pulled them towards the opening doors of the elevator which had just arrived. As the doors started to slide closed, Allissa made the face again. Again, the children giggled, a giggle that faded as the elevator started its ascent.

Stepping into the next available elevator, Leo pressed the button for the 8th floor and they began to rattle upwards.

Allissa caught Leo's eye with an expression in which she intended to say, *what sort of dingy place is this? Clearly failing to understand, Leo beamed in reply.*

The lift slowed to a stop. Then, with an age of incremental adjustments in height, the doors slid open.

Expecting a corridor that was as dark and decaying as the outside, Allissa was surprised when they stepped from the lift into daylight. Looking left and right she realised they were on a balcony which ran around an open space in the centre of the building. The gap was forty feet or so across and open to the deep blue sky above.

Stepping out onto the balcony, Allissa noticed women washing crockery or clothes in buckets, old men smoking and barefooted children chasing each other from the open door of one apartment to the next. Across the gap, colourful washing strung like bunting shimmered in the still air. Below, across a concrete wall at the edge of the balcony, Allissa saw the glass roof of the shopping mall and the balconies of the floors below. It was like a village hidden above the shopping centre in the middle of the city.

"This way," Leo said, setting off along the balcony. At first, Allissa felt intrusive; people's doors were open and inside they ate, cooked or snoozed. Passing four old men smiling through the yellow haze of their cigarette smoke, Allissa raised a hand in a wave of greeting and the men did the same.

In the small room used as a reception by their hotel, the receptionist took details, scanned passports, issued their key and sent them one floor up to another apartment which was part of the same hotel. Leo let them in then counted out the third door on the right. Unlocking the door, he pushed it open. The room was tiny. Just big enough for two single beds and a thin gap between them. Dropping her bag on one of the beds, Allissa headed straight for the bathroom.

"You have the first shower then," Leo said, sitting on the other creaking bed. They'd made it to Hong Kong. Now all they had to do was track down someone who didn't want to be found.

Chapter 36

Looking at herself in the office's washroom mirror, Isobel realised how hard the last few days had been. Beneath her eyes dark patches had started to appear and her pale skin had begun to blotch. Rummaging in her handbag, she pulled out a small make-up bag, unzipped it and began to re-apply. Isobel knew there was be a lot to learn, a lot to work out, but she hadn't realised it would be this much. Every night she stayed late in the office. Then, returning to her dingy hotel room, she continued working until long past midnight.

The problem was, Isobel couldn't tell anyone how much she needed to learn. She knew if she did, if she asked the wrong thing, questions would be asked. And if that happened, the dream would be over.

She was getting used to her vision swimming with tiredness. The haze that fatigue brought. It would get easier, she told herself. It *would* get easier. If she could just finish this one project then…

Tonight, Isobel was staying late for a different reason. Tonight she had a plan to guarantee her success. Although inexperienced at the job, Isobel wasn't helpless. She'd gotten this far and had what it took to succeed.

Finalising her lipstick and looking at herself in the mirror, she smiled. It was a shallow smile, one that didn't fool the woman who looked back at her. She'd wanted to get there through hard work alone but that was starting to feel impossible. There was just too much to learn.

Feeling her eyes prickle, Isobel's smile dropped. She wanted to be a great architect because of her eye for design, her skill with structure and invention, her flair for creativity and beauty. But all she saw looking back at her was a body, a body with all the curves in the right places. A body that people, particularly men, saw before all else. She had cursed it many times, but now, watching herself in the mirror, she was going to put it to good use.

She could get there through hard work alone, but why not use the other tools at her disposal?

Packing her make up away, Isobel pulled a blister pack of caffeine tablets from the bag, popped out two and swallowed. Then she rubbed moisturiser onto her hands, sprayed perfume on her chest and pulled her face into a compliant smile. *There's always more than one route to success,* she thought, pushing open the door and walking back into the open plan office.

The office was empty. The rest of the team had left hours ago.

Psyching herself up, Isobel sat back at her desk. Touching the mouse, the project sprung onto the screen.

She didn't have to wait long.

"You're working late," came a sibilant voice from behind her.

Isobel smiled to herself before turning, acting startled.

"I'm sorry, did I scare you?" Yee said softly, approaching her desk.

"Yes, I, I, I didn't realise there was anyone here," Isobel said, acting flustered.

"That's fine, it's normal for people to work late," Yee said, perching on the desk next to hers. "You're not expected to, though. If the work is too much or you're struggling, say something."

"It's, I'm, just trying to get my head around this project," Isobel said. "There's a lot to learn."

"I bet. Starting at a new place must be difficult. Is there anything I can help you with?" Yee leaned towards the screen.

"I think I've made a mess of the figures here," Isobel said, pointing. "Can't quite work the…"

Yee leaned in further.

"Yes, I see what you've done." Yee reached across and took the mouse. Isobel delayed moving her hand. Their skin brushed. Yee's touch felt cold.

Yee flicked through a couple of menus, changed some settings and then returned to the design screen.

"There you go, you just had it in the wrong view, easy mistake."

Isobel looked up towards him, her face reddening.

"I'm sorry," she said, fanning her face with slender fingers. "It's all just so much – I'm doing my best."

"It's fine, you're doing great. There is so much to learn at a new place. You're doing great, don't worry about it."

"It's just…" Isobel felt a tear streak her newly applied make up.

"Tell you what," Yee said. "Leave this now. It's a new system to you. I'll get one of the guys to give you a walk-through in the morning. Let's have a drink. I have something a little stronger than coffee in my office."

Isobel looked up at him, smiled weakly and nodded.

Chapter 37

Outside on the balconies people were readying themselves for the evening as the sky started to darken. The building quietened as running children were called in from their games and the washing was collected. As Leo and Allissa left their hotel room, the smell of sweet soy sauce and the sounds of Chinese bedtime stories carried from open doors in the still night air. There was a trust in the building that was unlike many of the cities the pair had visited before.

By the lifts, the old men continued to smoke. As Leo and Allissa approached they paused their conversation and smiled.

Leo wondered what it would feel like having new people always walking through your home like this. Would it be intrusive or intriguing? The residents here seemed used to it, as though the comings and goings of tourists was just part of their community. Just part of the life in the building.

Walking out onto Nathan Road, Leo was suddenly aware of the noises of the city. Traffic snarled on the wide road and the persistent hawkers continued to shout and jostle. The contrast to the peace of moments ago was startling.

"I love cities like this," Allissa said as they pushed through the crowds.

Despite the coming darkness, people bustled past. Cocktail traffic, dinner and drinks. The nocturnal carnival of the city.

Leo didn't share her excitement. There was too much mystery, too much unknown. Although Leo had been forced to face some of these fears in Kathmandu, he still found the people, the darkening streets and mysterious neon clad restaurants uncomfortable. Following Allissa, Leo reminded himself that they were here to do a job. They would get that done as quickly as possible and then go home.

Five minutes later, the pair walked into a dimly-lit bar. While Leo ordered two bottles of Tsingtau, Allissa found them a high table looking out into the street.

"Tomorrow then," Leo said after a long sip of the beer. "We will get to the building early, get a picture of Isobel going in, then it's job done. That's all we need. Easy stuff." He swigged again and saw Allissa smile.

"You don't think we should tell them she's a fraud?" Allissa said.

"Nope, we don't need to get involved."

"I'm not sure a picture is enough though. The court could argue that it's someone who looks similar. What if she's changed her appearance?"

"All we need is enough to get Jamie out. A picture should be enough."

"It *could* be enough," Allissa said, pausing as a motorbike thumped past the open front of the bar, filling the room with two-stroke fumes. "But I think we need to get a statement from the company too. We don't get paid if we don't get the proof that gets Jamie off remember. Do you really want to be coming back a second time?"

Leo tensed his face in thought. This was getting further

115

involved; they needed to keep it as simple as possible.

"We need them to say, 'Jamie Price started work here on this date and here's a CCTV image,' then it's job done. No getting out of that." Allissa said. She was right and Leo knew it.

"Sure, alright," he conceded, thinking for a moment. "Let's contact the director first thing in the morning, send him the article of Isobel in the newspaper so he can see what we're dealing with."

"Good idea. If he knows it's part of a murder investigation, he'll definitely pay attention."

"Then we can get it over to Jamie's lawyer tomorrow, and *then* we're done. We go home and we get paid." Leo said. Allissa took a thoughtful sip, a smile glinting in her eyes. Leo noticed it. He was learning that as much as he wanted them to, things rarely worked out like that. Life had a habit of interconnecting itself, twisting things around, muddling things up. If one thing changed, everything changed.

"If you say so," Allissa said, "but peoples' lives are complicated and once you get involved –"

"Nope," Leo said. "This one's simple. We get the confirmation, we get the photo, we send that off and then we're done. We don't even need to talk to Isobel – she can do what she likes."

Leo watched as Allissa sunk a third of the bottle. Although the things she found exciting scared him, Leo knew that when it mattered, she would be there. They'd both learned that the hard way.

"Have you learned from your mistakes with me then? About getting involved?" Allissa asked as though reading his mind.

"Yeah, live and learn," Leo said, a wry smile forming. "I suppose you're my greatest success." Finishing his beer, Leo

116

began to blush. "Professionally. My greatest professional success," he added.

Chapter 38

Two minutes later, Isobel let their hands brush past each other again as Yee handed her a glass.

"It's a good one this, single malt. Contractors donate it by the container load," Yee said, pouring himself one.

Yee's office was in near-darkness, low side lights illuminated the furniture.

"What do you normally drink?" he asked, lifting his own.

Isobel thought back to nights out at home; it all seemed like such a long time ago.

"Wine or cocktails," she said softly.

Through the window, the skyline of Hong Kong Island throbbed. Although most of the buildings were in darkness, the lights of the cars below reflected into a myriad of sparkles across their glass and chrome.

"It's beautiful, isn't it?" Yee said, noticing Isobel looking through the window. "First thing in the morning is my favourite time, before sunrise. But evening is great too."

"Yes, it's very beautiful. I can see why you have your office here."

Yee turned and smiled. They were both leaning against his desk now.

"It must be hard moving to a new city," he said. "I moved here when I was eighteen, to start this firm."

"You've done well with it," Isobel moved her glass to indicate the office.

"Thanks, it's been a passion."

Isobel slid to the left. Their shoulders were almost touching now. Light from the traffic moving in swathes down the boulevards below danced across the ceiling. Behind them, a cruise ship begun to slide across the gap in the towers. Its celebratory lights skipped across the water.

"Maybe one day you'll help me on a project like this," Yee said looking towards her, "like this building."

"I'd like that, I've always wanted to design something iconic."

Isobel let her eyes linger across his. He had to make the first move, that was key.

"It must be incredible to have such an impact on the world," Isobel said, turning her body slightly to face him. His eyes ran across her figure like the swirling lights of the cars below.

"Yes, it is," Yee said, putting his glass down on the table.

For a moment there was space between them.

In architecture, Isobel knew that the space between things is everything. The difference between perfection and disaster. But feeling Yee's cold hand on her waist, and seeing him move towards her, she also knew that space, or the lack of it, is control. That was what she needed, control.

There's no way he's getting rid of me now, she thought, smiling.

Chapter 39

They'll be there by now, Jamie thought, lying back on his prison bed. Light from the barred window fanned across the ceiling. It was never dark in his cell, but Jamie didn't mind.

He should be there by now, not in here. This should have been the making of his career, everything he had studied, worked and lived for.

The decisions lapped around his mind, everything that led to this moment, everything that had brought him here. How was he to know? How was he to know that she would do this?

Was it a case of being in the wrong place at the wrong time? Just kissing the wrong woman? Or was it more than that? Isobel knew that he was in here now, and yet she was letting him suffer. Why? What had he done to deserve this?

How could she put him through this?

He felt his fists ball in anger beneath the thin blanket.

He remembered Isobel in the car park – the way she'd switched emotions. The anger and pain that was so convincing and then a moment later was gone. She could be persuasive and compelling, he knew that. The problem was, no one else did. She could be anywhere, doing anything.

"I advise you to plead guilty." The words his lawyer had

spoken hours ago echoed through his mind. "You'll get a lighter sentence. The court will look favourably on your honesty. Say it was an accident."

"But I haven't done anything," Jamie said, again and again. "I did not kill her. I do not know where she is."

"Hair fibres were found on your clothes, and a patch of her blood was found in the boot of your car. How can you explain those things?"

"She must have put them there."

"Why would she want to do this? Why would she want to frame you for this?"

"You don't know her, she was angry. I don't know why. It started after it happened."

"After what happened?"

"After we slept together."

"Consensually?"

"Of course!"

"What about the complaints to HR? Unwanted advances."

The conversation spun in circles. Everything Jamie said was discounted or looked suspicious because of something she had said or done.

"Why would someone who had gone to the effort of complaining about you to HR sleep with you?"

"I don't know – but she did,"

"When did this happen?"

"At the Christmas party last year."

"Did anyone see you together?"

Jamie cast his mind back to the balcony above the city. The cold night air. The shapes in the smoke dancing behind them. Thudding music in the distance. Liquid words. The looks of promise and opportunity.

"I don't think so."

"I'm sure what you say is true," the lawyer said apologetically. "You're a good guy in a bad situation. A really bad situation. Nothing you say can be proved. But the prosecution, they have proof. That's what we need. Proof, evidence. Something that can't be muddied or confused. Otherwise you're better off just pleading guilty."

They'll be there by now. They are my only hope.

A voice down the corridor started to cry.

My only hope of getting out of here.

Once the noise started it got louder. The voice was joined by a banging. Not a repetitive thud, but a violent unpredictable strike between screams.

Jamie shut his eyes against the noise and hoped for the proof they needed.

Chapter 40

The banging started when Leo and Allissa had been asleep for an hour. It came from somewhere close. Lying in the darkness they couldn't work out exactly where. Then when the shouting started, they knew they wouldn't sleep again.

"What's that?" Allissa said, sitting up and rubbing a hand across her face. They heard the noise again, a loud bang echoing through the structure of the building followed by raised voices in a language they didn't understand.

"I'm not sure," Leo said sleepily from the darkness. "They'll shut up soon."

But they didn't; another bang, another shout. More aggressive this time.

Allissa reached over and switched on the light. It stung her eyes as she pulled herself up in bed.

"We're not getting involved," Leo said, watching Allissa get up and pull a hoodie over the baggy t-shirt she was wearing.

"Sure, just going to see."

Letting themselves out of the room, they walked towards the balcony. The corridor between the rooms was dark.

At the door leading out to the balcony, the pair stopped. Allissa was first, resting her hand on the door and leaning close. Another crash. A faint wailing. The noise was nearby now. Depressing the handle, Allissa heard the lock disengage.

"Slowly," Leo said. "Careful." There was frustration or fear in his voice. In the darkness Allissa couldn't tell which.

"Course," she said, pushing the door open.

Outside, the balconies were still lit but most of the apartments seemed to be in darkness.

They heard another bang. It was close. They didn't have to wait long.

A moment later, the door to the right flew open and four people stumbled out. Allissa recognised them as the family that lived there, a man, a woman and two children. Behind them, forcing them from the apartment, stood three solid-looking men.

The children sobbed mercilessly and held the hands of their mother. The father, desperate at the state of his family tried to force his way back in. He was easily overpowered and pushed back out. He stumbled across the balcony, collided with the wall and slid to the floor. Seeing this, the family's wailing amplified.

Allissa looked at the children, their faces screwed-up in fear. Their eyes streaked with tears. One of them wore their top inside out.

She recognised them as the children and woman they'd seen waiting for the lift a few hours before. They'd smiled and giggled at her. Shy but inquisitive. Now desperate and if her assessment was correct, newly homeless.

Watching in silence, Allissa saw the three thick-necked men leave the apartment. The last to leave turned off the lights, pulled the door shut and locked it with a padlock and chain. Then, tucking the key inside his jacket, he considered the family once more before walking away.

As the men neared the elevators, their bulky shapes becoming part of the gloom, Allissa couldn't help but think she saw them smiling.

Allissa and Leo exchanged looks of silent shock. This family had just been thrown from their home in the middle of the night wearing nothing more than a few clothes. Watching from the door they felt helpless, powerless.

"We need to help," Allissa whispered at Leo. "We can't just leave them here."

"Wait... watch," Leo said, as two lights further down the corridor clicked on, then a third and a fourth. Then a woman appeared from her door carrying a thick blanket. Approaching the family, she wrapped it around the children and hugged the mother. Another woman appeared with a warm top which she put on one of the children. And another with a top for the other child. Then on the opposite balcony a door opened. From it a man beckoned the family towards him.

"This happens all the time," a Chinese-accented voice said from behind them. Startled at the voice, Allissa turned. A girl who couldn't be more than a teenager stood beside them.

"The owners of the building want to re-develop it to make expensive apartments," the girl said. "They cannot force us to leave – that's illegal, so they have increased the rent four times in the last year. That is also illegal," she said, "but because they are not physically forcing anyone, they get away with it. We think the owner is bribing someone to ignore it, as we have complained again and again but no one listens. This happens very often when families just cannot pay."

Allissa watched the family as they entered their neighbour's apartment and the door closed behind them. At least tonight they had somewhere to stay.

The girl who had spoken to them disappeared and the windows around the balcony started to darken. Silence once again fell over the vertical village.

Allissa and Leo made their way back inside too, closing the door on the events they'd seen.

Later, lying awake, Allissa remembered something Leo had said a few months before, "you don't see the world when you travel, but you feel it."

Chapter 41

Waking earlier than usual, Isobel smiled to herself. It wasn't the grime-covered furniture of the room that made her smile, or the stained sheets she had at first despised but was starting to get used to, it was the events of the previous evening.

Now, she knew, sitting up in bed and looking towards the window, she was indispensable.

Across the window, made translucent with the filth of neglect, the shadow of one of the street's neon signs fell. It was a world away from the view from the office last night when she had let Yee kiss her.

If Isobel believed in such a thing, she would have thought it romantic.

The whispered words, as though something secret, private, sexy was going on.

The lights of the traffic below swirling across the ceiling. Then, with her lips parted, a smile playing at the corners, Isobel had looked straight at him and let him close the gap.

Afterwards, Yee had seemed almost apologetic, but she'd silenced that with another kiss. His hands explored her body briefly. She didn't mind. That was just going to make it better.

Isobel knew Yee was married. Married his high school

sweetheart it had said in one of the newspaper interviews she'd read.

"I really should be going, it's really late," she'd said, her eyes lingering on Yee for a moment too long.

He'd fumbled some reply and shown her back through to the deserted reception, as though she didn't know the way.

Then, Isobel laughing to herself at the genius of it all, had paused and looked back at him. Like a hungry puppy, Yee had walked across to her, stretched up and kissed her again.

Things were starting to go her way, Isobel thought, getting out of bed.

"Mr Yee," she said to herself, looking at the depressing room and imagining a conversation she was going to have when she got to the office later. "How's my apartment coming on?"

Chapter 42

Tower 21 stretched upwards in Hong Kong's milky pre-dawn. The tops of the buildings were mere rumours, drowned in the mist which had rolled in from the sea.

As Leo and Allissa emerged from the metro station, it felt as though the sun was there somewhere, threatening to burst through at any moment.

They found Tower 21 easily. It was two minutes' walk from the station. The building was a square construction of dark windows and chrome details, all running skyward to a tapered point. Despite the early hour, light radiated from every floor. Leo squinted upwards towards the offices of OZ Architecture which occupied the 21st floor. In most cities, Tower 21 would have been considered a tall building. On Hong Kong Island though, it was belittled by its neighbours and The Peak which lay somewhere behind the mist.

Walking past, Allissa looked into the opulent reception area. Black marble floors gleamed beneath bright hanging lights. A reception desk sat in the middle and a bank of eight elevators waited expectantly. Fortunately, there was only one way in, meaning Isobel would have to cross the plaza in front of the tower.

"We need to keep moving," Leo said, "otherwise people in there will get suspicious." He pointed into the reception desk where the day shift security guard had just turned up to relieve the tired-looking night man.

"We'll walk up to the end of the plaza there and back again," Leo indicated the trickle of people already heading from the station, "that way she'll have to pass one of us. Make sure you're ready for the photo."

Within a few minutes the trickle of stone-faced people flowing from the station had become a stream. As light seeped further into the sky, it became a torrent.

"I don't think this is going to work," Allissa said after they'd been walking backwards and forwards for almost an hour. "There's too many people, we could easily miss her. No one will notice us now anyway."

Leo agreed.

"I'll wait by the station entrance. You wait by the tower. That way we've got two chances." Turning back towards the station, Allissa tried to keep the picture of Isobel in her mind.

Red hair, pale skin, tall, slender, pretty.

Another train arrived somewhere beneath the road. A herd of people surged upwards. Allissa scanned them from the top of the stairs. Isobel had to be here somewhere.

Red hair, pale skin, tall, slender, pretty.

On the other side of the gushing bodies, a tall woman made her way up the stairs. It could be Isobel, but Allissa wasn't sure.

Not wanting the woman to slip by, even if it wasn't Isobel, Allissa raised her phone and aimed the camera. Stepping forward to get the angle right, Allissa moved into the stream of pushing bodies.

"Watch out!" someone shouted as they walked into Allissa, ruining the photo and knocking her phone to the floor.

"Some people," came another voice, "they can be so rude. Here, let me help you." The voice's owner, a woman, crouched to pick up the phone, "I hope it's not broken."

"I don't think so," Allissa said, looking down at the pale, slender hands that held the phone. "Thank you." Taking it, Allissa looked at the woman for the first time. A pretty face framed with red hair.

Recognition dropped.

Isobel.

It was her.

Allissa knew it.

Fumbling with the phone, Allissa watched Isobel turn and push back into the stream of people.

She'd missed the shot. She'd been too slow.

Allissa started after her. They needed this photograph.

Isobel was four people ahead as Allissa tried to take a photo. It just showed the red hair. It proved nothing.

Leo had better be paying attention.

But Leo was on the right, on the wrong side of the torrent of people to get a clear shot. Pushing out to the left, Allissa saw Leo hold up his phone and take the picture. But there were too many people between them for a good shot. It wouldn't be clear enough. It wasn't going to happen.

Barging forwards and cutting a corner, Allissa got in front. She turned her phone round and took a picture of the people walking behind. No time to check. This needed to be right, it was down to her.

Tower 21's automatic doors had no time to slide closed as the stream of people entered. Allissa could feel the cool of the air-conditioner as she pushed into the building. This whole case relied on getting a good, provable photograph.

Allissa followed the stream of people into the foyer, her informal clothes and frantic expression belying her intentions to try and fit in. Then, stepping out of the crowd heading for the lift, she waited. All ideas of subtlety evaporated in her need for the picture.

Seconds later, Isobel passed, eyes forward. Allissa fired off five shots of her side profile. These were the pictures. They had to come out. A man's freedom hung in the balance.

Chapter 43

The early morning mist had cleared, leaving the towers of Hong Kong in striking contrast to the surrounding grid of blue sky.

Yee watched the city from his office on the top floor of Tower 21. The tangled web of light through the buildings of chrome and glass cut a web of shadows in the bright morning sun. He loved the misty Hong Kong mornings. Sometimes, arriving in his office at five as he did every day, the city appeared to be floating on the mist – like a city in the clouds. Normally the view brought him great happiness, but not this morning.

Drinking the dark, bitter coffee he had flown in from Istanbul, Yee let his mind run through the ten years he'd spent in this office. His business had done well, grown on the reputation of using the best people he could find from around the world. Clients used his firm because of their reputation, their attention to detail, their ability to turn the banal into the incredible, the everyday into the extraordinary.

Turning from the window, Yee looked around his office. This was the reason he'd got the place. Although, this morning the walls seemed to be closing in on him.

Running a hand through his hair, Yee looked at the painting

on the opposite wall. An original Kandinsky. He knew that to the untrained eye it looked like a mess of colours and shapes, lines, blobs and circles. It was only when you focused on it, analysed it, got inside it, that you could see order in the chaos. First seeing it in a gallery as a young man, Yee had been struck by it straight away. He found it inspiring. There was a lot going on, but to him it had just one clear meaning, one that he had dedicated his life to. Destruction and rebirth. Demolition and recreation. Taking something old and from it producing something new. That to him was beautiful, that was what it meant to be an architect.

Five years ago, hearing it was for sale, he had bought it for an exorbitant sum that made him wince a little even now.

Examining the curves and colours, letting them swim as his eyes lost focus, Yee thought of the e-mail he'd just received. It bothered him. A serious accusation against one of his staff. The new girl, she'd only started a few days ago. It was a shame, especially considering the events of the previous night.

Thinking about it made him uncomfortable; why did it have to be her?

He had been ready to palm it off as timewasters until he saw the attachments. One, a photograph of a UK tabloid newspaper showing a story about a missing woman, presumed to have been murdered by a jealous lover. The other, a grainy picture of his new member of staff entering the office. He had to admit they did look very similar.

This was a worry. He didn't need the bad publicity.

"Your ten o'clock appointment is here Mr Yee," came the voice of his receptionist from the door.

Yee ruffled his fingers through his hair again, roughing it at the sides then stroking it back into place.

It really was a worry.

* * *

The first thing that struck Leo, entering Yee's office, was the view. It was impressive.

Pulling his eyes from it, Leo watched the architect walk from behind his large desk to greet them. Despite a smile, Leo could see worry twitching at the sides of his mouth.

"Please take a seat," Yee said, guiding Leo and Alissa towards the chairs in the corner and then sitting with his back to the window. Leo wondered if Yee had directed them to the informal chairs as a conscious attempt to relax the situation. Conversations like this were as much about power as information.

Although small in stature, Yee's expensive suit and glinting watch hinted at power beyond the physical. Dropping into the seat, Leo realised he had to squint to see the architect clearly against the thick morning light which poured through the window. Yee was clearly a clever and manipulative man.

"Thank you for agreeing to see us, Mr Yee," Allissa said, undeterred.

"Would you like a drink before we begin?" Yee said.

Leo and Allissa had bought two cups of coffee and a pastry each in the coffee shop opposite as they waited for Yee's reply to their e-mail. Leo already had a headache from the caffeine.

"No, thank you," he said.

"In short," Allissa continued, "we've come here to avoid you having some kind of public scandal."

"We're on your side," Leo said. "We just need this to be sorted out."

Yee didn't reply but rubbed his short, quick fingers through the back of his hair.

"Our client," Leo began, leaning forward, "is a *man* called Jamie Price."

Yee nodded.

"He should be working for you here now, but instead he's in prison in London charged with murder."

There was a moment of silence, Leo let the words hang.

"Well, I don't see how…" Yee started before a thought caught up with him, "I don't know this Jamie Price. I've never met him."

"The problem is," Allissa asserted, "Jamie Price *has* come to work for you."

"Yes, she started last week," Yee said. "There must be more than one in the world?"

"Of course," Allissa said. Yee looked confident. "But I'm afraid it's not that simple."

"Mr Yee," Leo got his phone from his pocket and leaned forward, "let me show you something that'll make this very clear. As you saw in the e-mail we sent you this morning, this is the person you believe to be Jamie Price. We know she is working for you right now as this was taken this morning."

Yee nodded.

"And this," Leo scrolled to the picture of the newspaper article, "is a woman in the UK who is believed to have been murdered."

"Yes, I've seen these," Yee said. "They just look similar, it doesn't prove anything."

"This is the man who is in prison," Leo scrolled to the picture of Jamie. "He was supposed to be here working for you now. And here," Leo flicked to the picture of Isobel they had found online, "is the woman he is supposed to have murdered. The woman who you know as Jamie Price is actually Isobel Clark. She's been missing for a number of weeks and a man is in prison charged with her murder."

Leo thought he saw understanding fall over the architect's face.

"Feel free to do your own research into this when we've gone," Allissa said, "but we're here to help you, not accuse you."

"You're sure?" Yee asked. "There's no mistake?"

"No mistake," Allissa said. "Isobel has framed an innocent man for murder and is now working for you. She's a very manipulative woman."

Yee exhaled slowly.

"The way we see this," Allissa reassured, "this is not your fault. You've been conned by this woman as much as everyone else."

"I'm not sure the press will see it that way," Leo interjected.

"Our concern is the innocent man in prison, not Isobel or whatever you call her," Allissa said.

"But it wouldn't look good if it did come out," Leo reminded him.

"What do you need from me?" Yee asked.

"We need a timestamped CCTV image of her in this office. She needs to be in it clearly so the judge can see it's her. A statement from you saying when she started at your company and any other information you might hold on her. UK address, bank details etc."

"Then you'll make this go away?" Yee asked. "And nothing will come of it?"

"If we have those things today," Allissa said, "this goes no further."

"You could even be praised as the people who finally caught up with her," Leo added. "Not the company who hid someone illegally."

Yee thought for a few moments. Leo noticed him look behind them at something on the wall. Turning, he saw the painting, some modern orange swirly thing.

Seeming to wake, Yee pulled his phone from the inside pocket of his jacket. Pressing it a few times, he held it to his ear and barked some commands. Seconds later, a stocky Chinese man came through the door, a strong physique showing through his dark suit. Leo thought he looked familiar but wasn't sure how.

"This is Jiao," Yee said. "He sorts things out for me."

The two men spoke in what Leo assumed must be Cantonese for a minute.

"The picture please," Yee said, holding his hand out to Leo. Leo pulled it up onto the screen of his phone and passed it over.

The conversation restarted with more animated gestures, then there was a silence. The two men smiled at each other. Leo wished he could understand what they were saying.

"Jiao will prepare the video for you now," Yee said, as the burly man walked from the room. "Leave your contact details and we will send it over later today along with the other things you need."

Allissa and Leo stood.

"I am glad you have come to me on this matter, we will sort this out," Yee said, bowing slightly and smiling.

"Thank you for your help," Leo said. "All we want is to see an innocent man go free."

Walking to the door, Allissa paused. "What will you do about Isobel?"

Leo shot a look towards her. This was not part of their plan.

"She will no longer be working with us – I can assure you of that."

"You've done the right thing," Leo interjected. "It could have been pretty messy if your clients had found out."

"Yes, indeed, I want to avoid that at all costs. If there is anything you need while in Hong Kong, please let me know," Yee said, his smile broadening. "Perhaps dinner, or a nice hotel?"

Allissa sighed. Leo knew she was thinking of their tiny room in the high-rise village.

"We don't need anything," Leo said. "Just what we have discussed. Thank you."

"Yes, of course," Yee said, bowing again and indicating the door.

"Ohh, Kandinski," Allissa said, looking towards the painting. "Composition VII, one of my favourites; everything will come to an end, and then be reborn."

As Allissa and Leo crossed the open plan office, Yee watched them in silent surprise. How had the girl interpreted that from the painting? How had she seen what every single member of his team had failed to?

Shaking his head to regain focus, Yee turned and shut the door. He now had a problem, but with that had come a solution. A solution he looked forward to very much. From destruction would come rebirth. From chaos, Yee was going to bring order. Order where he was in charge.

Chapter 44

O'Leary's Irish Bar was dark as Leo and Allissa walked in. The brightness of the city swamped the room for a few seconds as they opened the door and then died as it closed behind them. Leo always wondered why Irish bars seemed to have a uniform style across the globe, dark wood panelling adorned with paintings of horses and landscapes. The dozen or so beer pumps and the back-bar mirror glimmered dreamily.

"What was that about the painting in Yee's office?" Leo asked as they stood at the bar. The place was empty, it was still before midday, but as far as Leo was concerned their work was done. He intended to sort flights home later that afternoon.

"Kandinski's composition VII. All about making order from chaos, apparently. Did a module in modern art at college."

"Do you think it's the real one?" Leo asked.

"It's possible. It wouldn't be cheap, but Yee clearly is a guy who has some money to spend."

"Yeah," Leo said thoughtfully as the barman approached. The sleeves of his grey shirt were rolled up and a dish cloth was draped across his shoulder.

"You're here early," he said in a lilting Irish accent. "What can I get you?"

Allissa ordered breakfast and beer.

"It'll be five o'clock at home," she said, looking at the reflection of a clock in the mirror.

"They're not pints," Leo said, watching the barman fill two glasses.

"500ml," the barman said, putting the glasses on fresh beer mats.

"George Orwell predicted this," Leo said grumpily, "and look how that turned out."

"Beer is beer," Allissa said, raising it to her lips, "and this one's good, thank you."

Sitting in a booth at the back of the bar and tasting the first sip of beer, Leo felt himself relax.

"Well, we did it," he said, lifting his pint to toast Allissa's. "Well done."

Allissa didn't look so sure as they clinked glasses.

"Well, yeah, as soon as we get the stuff from Yee we've got enough to get Jamie off. But it doesn't feel finished to me. Why did Isobel do it and what's she going to do now?"

"Don't worry about that," Leo said. "We've done the job we've been paid for. We can enjoy being in the city for a couple of days and then go home."

Privately Leo hoped they would be back sooner than that. The episode with his sister before they left, and their other cases made him want to be at home as soon as possible.

"But who really is Isobel and what caused her to do what she has?"

"We really don't need to worry about her," Leo said. "She decided to do the wrong thing and now that's come back to bite her. She clearly wasn't that worried about other people.

An innocent guy has spent weeks in prison because of her."

"Well yes, true," Allissa said. "But we all make bad decisions sometimes. I really think we should…"

Allissa stopped as her phone bleeped from the tabletop. The e-mail received icon glowed on the screen. Picking up and unlocking the phone, she saw it was from Yee.

Putting the drink down, Allissa opened the e-mail and read it aloud. As requested, it gave the dates Jamie or Isobel had worked at the firm, her previous address, passport information and some other details. A video file was also attached.

"They're presumably just the details of the real Jamie Price," Allissa said. "Just no one thought to check."

Tapping the video file, an image of the office's reception area filled the screen. In the corner the date and time were displayed. Allissa recognised it as 7:45 on the day Isobel started at the firm.

Watching closely, Allissa saw Isobel appear in the reception area. The receptionist must have been on the phone as Isobel stood for a few seconds and looked around the office.

"That'll do it," Allissa said, saving a screenshot of Isobel as she turned to face the camera. "We'll get that straight over to the lawyer. We will send the whole video as well, but that shot just says it all."

"Yep," Leo said. "Date and time, there she is, signed and sealed."

On the screen the receptionist finished her call and started to talk to Isobel. After exchanging a few words, Isobel sat on one of the chairs still in view of the camera. She crossed her legs and looked at something inside her bag.

"She looks a bit nervous, don't you think?" Leo said.

"Yeah. You would be though. Wouldn't you? I just don't understand," Allissa said, wondering out loud. "Surely she knew she wouldn't get away with it?"

As Allissa spoke, Yee walked into the shot. With no sound on the video, Leo and Allissa could only guess what they were saying. Nothing looked unusual.

"Well that's that done anyway," Leo said getting to his feet. "I'm going to sort out our next pressing issue." Allissa looked up at him.

"These glasses need filling," Leo held up the empty glasses. "We're celebrating. A job well done."

As Leo walked to the bar, Allissa turned back to the video. She had a rising sense of unease about this. Did anyone else even know Isobel was here? That put here in a very vulnerable position.

On the screen, Yee had taken a step towards Isobel who was now standing. Allissa watched as Yee pointed Isobel in the direction of his office. As Isobel began to walk, Yee turned to look at her, his face contorted into a smile as his eyes scanned her body. As the video cut out, the look on Yee's face stayed in Allissa's mind. It took her a few moments to realise where she had seen that face before, that look of smug entitlement. Then she realised, it was the look of someone who thought they could do what they like and not get caught. At that, Allissa's sense of unease grew further still.

Chapter 45

Yee stood behind his desk looking out at the city. This afternoon, the view brought him no pleasure. He poured another strong measure of single malt into a glass and sipped it greedily. As the hours had passed his anger had risen. How could someone think they would get away with that? Get away with cheating him, with playing him?

He was going to show Isobel how he treated liars. This was his city. People here played by his rules. And those that didn't? Jiao had a skill for those very effectively.

He picked up his phone and made two calls. The first to Jiao, the second to the receptionist telling her to call Jamie into his office.

Jamie or Isobel or whatever your name actually is.

Things like this weren't supposed to happen. Jamie had a great CV, the ideal qualifications, excellent experience. Yee had thought the recruitment agency did well securing her at a good price. They'd done the interview and the checks, all he had to do was pay. That he'd done gladly knowing the experience that would be joining his firm. Yee had felt lucky to get her.

And then she'd arrived, efficient, hardworking, and, well he had to admit it, beautiful. Yee shook his head, trying to remove the thought of how good her body had felt last night. Looking down at the screen of his laptop, he saw her picture displayed as part of a newspaper article. It was a good picture, her hair was swept over one shoulder as she looked into the camera, her lips a deep red.

He'd noticed her figure on that first day, from a distance to start with. Thinking back, Yee pictured her. She knew what she was doing. She knew the effect she was having.

Turning to look at the Kandinsky, Yee grew irritated. Had he gone soft? Had he let standards slip? No. He wouldn't let standards slip. Not for her, not for anyone. It didn't matter how beautiful she was. How good her warm skin felt under his touch. How young and fragrant and keen...

Yee was shaken from his thoughts by the sound door opening.

Turning, he saw that figure. Isobel. She smiled at him. She had no idea.

"You asked for me?" Isobel said, walking confidently towards him.

Yee stole a glance at her before turning back towards the window. There would be plenty of time for that body to be his.

Looking out at the whispering city, Yee took a sip of the whiskey. Isobel wouldn't be having any this time.

"You know Isobel, I never get bored of this view."

For a moment there was silence. The traffic below seeped through the city and somewhere an air conditioner murmured.

"You're right, it's very beautiful," Isobel replied.

Yee stood still, his back to Isobel as a grin spread across his face.

145

As Yee turned, Isobel realised her mistake.

"I'm sorry, I didn't hear what you just said. What did you mean? I..."

Yee held up a hand to stop her. Her complexion betrayed any credibility. Her eyes darted left and right.

Slowly, Yee took a swallow of the spirit and drew a deep breath. Control regained. Order from chaos.

"This gives me a problem," Yee said, fixing Isobel with a stare. "I know you're not the person you're supposed to be."

"I... I..." Isobel stuttered, but again Yee silenced her with a look.

"Someone brought this to my attention," Yee said, turning the laptop.

Isobel looked down at the screen and seemed to pale in recognition of her own face staring back at her beneath the headline *Man Arrested for Murder.*

"It's a shame you're so... how shall I say... pleasing to the eye."

Yee didn't bother to hide his eyes roaming her body now.

Isobel stood still, gulping back panic.

"If you'd been more, say, plain, I bet they wouldn't have bothered with your picture."

Isobel gripped the desk for support, her knuckles draining of colour.

"It's funny though," Yee continued, "how you thought you could get away with it. How long did you think it would take people to notice? I suppose," he took a sip of the drink, "I'm a little disappointed. Especially after last night. But..."

"I'll go," Isobel interrupted suddenly, as though regaining control. "I'll go now. You won't see me again."

"No," Yee said, a hand crashing to the table, stopping Isobel

146

in mid-turn. "We need to talk. You see, I wonder if there is anyone who actually knows you're here?"

"I didn't mean to deceive you," Isobel said, backing away. "I'm sorry if that's upset you. You won't see me again," she repeated, taking another step.

No, Yee thought. She was not in control now, he was.

"You know you are committing fraud," Yee said, louder as Isobel took a step towards the door. "That's a major crime here in Hong Kong."

"I have nothing to say," Isobel said dismissively, turning away from Yee to face the door. "I'll collect my things and go now."

"Do you know," Yee said, noticing Isobel's hand on the door handle, "what the prisons are like here?"

She paused.

"Well I won't give you too much detail, but they'll make the prison your friend is in seem like luxury. And for what you've done, you could end up spending quite a long time in one."

Isobel turned. Her flushed skin shone under the bright lights.

"I'm just suggesting we have a conversation, that's all," Yee said sweetly, taking a sip of the diminishing whiskey. "I'm sure we can sort this out like adults."

"No," Isobel said after a pause. Then she turned, pulled open the door and stepped into the wide arms and barrel-shaped chest of Jiao.

"I bet he's shitting it now," Allissa said looking at the picture of Yee she had saved.

"He looked at this girl?" Leo said. "So what? We don't know anything."

"Yeah but it's more than that, I've seen this look before." Allissa pointed at the phone. "I bet you something has happened. He's the sort of guy who gets what he wants. Is he married?"

Leo reluctantly read Yee's biography from his phone.

"Married and lives with his wife and two daughters in the Hong Kong Mid-Levels area."

Allissa exhaled slowly.

"He owns OZ Architecture and a number of restaurants and apartments in Hong Kong," Leo read. "He has a number of awards including one for the design of The Address, a residential tower in the mid-levels area which was opened to much acclaim last year. Yee is the patron of two charities and was crowned Hong Kong's businessman of the year three years ago. And ultimately," Leo continued closing the website, "it's nothing to do with us. We've found Isobel, we've done our job. It's time to have a beer and then go home."

Leo lay his phone face down on the table and sat back in

the booth.

"You've got to be joking," Allissa said, tilting her head forward. "We're involved now."

"No, we've done our job. This is their mess, we're not being paid to sort it out."

"Yes, but Isobel could be in danger, or if something has gone on, Yee could be in danger. Either one of them could blackmail the other. We need to see this through."

"No, that's all their doing. If Yee has done something, then that's up to him. As for Isobel she's been stupid and now has to live with the consequences. If either of them wants to hire us they can. But at the moment," Leo paused for a sip of his beer, "we are done."

"Yes, but there's so much more here," Allissa said. "Don't you want to know –"

"No," Leo snapped. "We can't get involved in everyone else's issues. What Yee and Isobel may or may not have done is their problem. Not ours. They don't need us messing around when we have paying customers wanting our help. And my sister being in a –" Leo stopped, realising he had raised his voice louder than he intended. "Look," he said softly, "it's their issue, not ours, we've done a good job, let's celebrate."

Allissa brooded across the table at Leo, sipping her pint and scanning through the CCTV video again. Leo sat back and let his eyes close. He knew he was right and wouldn't be persuaded.

"We've done well," Leo repeated five minutes later. "We've found what we were looking for, now let's enjoy Hong Kong and have some more of this." He held the glass up into the light. It was almost finished; 500mls really wasn't very much.

"And talk to Yee tomorrow," Allissa said, getting up, picking up the empty glasses and taking them to the bar.

Sometimes there was no arguing with her Leo thought, watching Allissa walk away. Letting his eyes close again, Leo's chest tightened at the echoes of a memory.

***

Mya walks away from him down the jetty towards their cabin in Kao Tao. It's the single event that has led him here. As her silhouette fades, leaving him sitting on the ocean's edge, waves splashing his heels, he looks up at a universe of possibilities in the darkening sky.

"You know the stars," Mya had said minutes before. "They're actually visions from the past."

"What do you mean?"

"They're so far away, the light takes so long to get here that what we see now actually happened years ago."

"So they're like memories?"

"Yeah, I suppose, just other people's memories."

What Leo didn't know, what he couldn't have known, was that she was going to disappear from him under those very stars. He didn't know that it would be years until he saw her again.

Chapter 47

Isobel leapt back after colliding with the man in the doorway. She'd seen him around the office, his thick arms barely contained by his jacket.

"Excuse me," she said, looking at him. His face contorted into an unnatural grin.

He didn't move. Behind him, Isobel could see the open plan office space was empty. It was lunchtime and her colleagues would be off getting artisan paninis or green smoothies from the café on the tenth floor.

"Excuse me, I need to get past," Isobel said again. Fear welled through her. The man shook his head and took a step forward, arms by his sides, pushing her back into Yee's office.

"Get out the way," Isobel yelled, pushing a shoulder into his chest. It felt like a brick wall beneath his shirt.

The man took another step forward and pulled the door shut behind him.

Panic rising, Isobel raised a hand towards his face. It was intercepted by a thick fist which closed around her wrist like a vice.

"No, get off, let me…" Isobel wriggled and screamed as the man, using just his grip on one wrist, forced her across the room to one of the chairs by the window.

As she was pushed down into it, Isobel looked across at Yee.

"What are you... you won't..." she said. Yee held up a hand to silence her.

"We just need to have a little conversation. There's no need for all this childish messing about..."

Isobel, realising the futility of her wriggling, settled down.

"If you're going to behave properly..." Yee said, to which Isobel didn't respond. She looked at the floor, eyebrows bunched.

Yee said something to the man. Who, hearing the instruction, let go of her wrist. Isobel's arm dropped into her lap. She rubbed it with the other hand, sore from his grip.

"Listen," Yee said, crouching to the floor in her eyeline. "We just need to have a conversation about this. We can sort it out like adults."

Isobel looked away, refusing to meet Yee's eye.

"I don't want you to go to prison," Yee continued, grinning. Isobel glanced at him. "I want us to work this out... like we started to last night."

Isobel felt Yee's hand on her leg just above the knee and shuddered. It felt cold as he moved it up her thigh beneath her skirt.

Isobel tried to push Yee's hands away. Jiao got there first, grabbing her wrist again.

"Look," Yee whispered, his hand continuing upwards. "I can be very secretive. There's no reason anything has to change. I'm enjoying your company."

Isobel tried to stand as Yee's hand reached its destination. Two meaty palms came down across her shoulders and forced her back into the seat.

"I only want a little more than you've already given me," Yee

152

said. "And you did that all by yourself."

Isobel suppressed a sob.

"I'll make you a deal," Yee said leaning forwards, his mouth against her cheek. Isobel could smell whiskey on his breath.

"You do what you're told. You keep your job. You get the apartment. The life you want. You just have to come to me when you're called."

Isobel didn't move. Her chest felt tight. With each inhalation she felt closer to breaking down altogether.

"We'll start now," Yee said, standing and undoing his belt. "Jiao will be waiting just outside. I think you'll behave."

Isobel looked up at the little man, his face reddened by alcohol and excitement. Breathing for what felt like the first time in minutes, she looked around the office. Jiao had gone.

Through the window the city whispered. Inside Isobel screamed.

Chapter 48

There are many ways to get from Kowloon across to Hong Kong Island. There are taxis and buses which round the harbour and take one of the bridges across the water, the metro which takes a direct route beneath the waves, but the most picturesque has to be the Star Ferry. These antique boats shuttle between the Island and Kowloon from long before dawn until after dusk. The Ferries serve as a connection for tourists wanting a different perspective on the city, or locals not wanting to endure the claustrophobia of the peak-time metro.

One of the most spectacular times, Leo thought as he looked back across the shimmering water at the multicoloured towers of Hong Kong, has got to be after dark. After the crowds have dispersed from the evening light show, and the floating restaurants have started to return to their moorings. When the city is starting to relax itself into a disturbed calm for a few hours.

Leo and Allissa had spent numerous hours in the Irish bar on Hong Kong Island. After sending the e-mail to Jamie's lawyer and receiving confirmation that he too thought it would be enough to tip the balance in Jamie's favour, they had something to celebrate. Or certainly, Leo thought they had something to celebrate. Allissa had been reluctant to start with, but as the drinks flowed, she had seemed to start enjoying herself.

As darkness veiled the city, they'd moved to a different bar where a band played covers of western pop music.

For Leo, watching Allissa on the dancefloor, it was a well-needed night of relaxation.

For Allissa, it was simply a distraction. She knew she would tie up the loose ends with or without Leo's help.

Leo felt content with the way the case had gone. They'd come to Hong Kong, found the person they were looking for and would be paid well for it. It was exactly the sort of case he hoped to see more of as the business's reputation grew.

Now, watching the lights of the island skip across the inky water, Leo looked down at Allissa at the railing to his right. He knew Allissa found it hard to walk away from loose ends. He knew that Allissa would no doubt call Yee the following day, whether he wanted her to or not.

"Do you really think we need to check up on Isobel?" Leo said, watching the lights from the shore pattern across Allissa's face.

"Yes, we should find out what's happening and check everyone is alright."

"OK," Leo said, the warmth of alcohol melting his earlier resolve. "We will get Isobel's number from Yee and just check she's ok. Would that be enough?"

Allissa looked up at him and nodded.

"Good," Leo said, sliding along the railing until his elbow touched Allissa's. Ignoring his impulse to put his arm around her – they were just friends – Leo thought about that phone call. Isobel would either be abusive because they had ruined her plans or would already have fled the city. Either way, as he watched the horizon dance, Leo was confident that the job was done.

Chapter 49

The apartment was just as Yee had promised. Although when Jiao opened the door and shoved Isobel inside, the view across to the Hong Kong island or the stirring lights of Kowloon below gave her no pleasure. When Jiao closed the door and a key churned in the lock, Isobel felt sick. What had she got herself into now?

Earlier in Yee's office, Isobel hadn't known whether to fight or scream. Half of her thought that she wouldn't let him anywhere near her, she would fight and tear and scratch with all the strength she had. The other half thought that would only make it last longer and increase his sense of superiority, his feeling of power, when eventually she was overpowered.

Sitting there, Isobel had tasted the acid burn in her throat as she stifled a sob. She knew she'd made mistakes, acted unfairly, but she didn't deserve this. She didn't.

Isobel had tried not to watch Yee undoing his belt, walking towards her. She had tried to focus on something else. Ignoring him felt like taking away some of his power. As he neared, Isobel had closed her eyes tight and drew a deep breath.

She wouldn't open them until it was over.

All she could hear was her hot breath singing in her lungs.

Then a phone rang.

Yee grumbled, belt buckle jangling, over to his desk. Isobel opened her eyes to see him talking into the phone, his back to her.

Hanging up, he turned and smiled.

"I'm sorry about that. I'm afraid we're going to have to delay this," Yee said. "Such a shame but I have a family commitment I need to attend."

Isobel took a deep breath, not realising how long it had been since the last one.

"Jiao will look after you, I think your apartment is almost ready. He'll take you there, just to make sure you're safe. Then tomorrow we can resume the fun."

Isobel wasn't sure what time it was when they'd got to the apartment, but it was still light. Some time since, Jiao had delivered her a bag of clothes and some food. Isobel had eaten hungrily and then pulled the clothes from the bag. They had been bought especially; the tags still attached.

Again, Isobel tried the door. Locked.

She returned to the window and looked out across the city. The sun had fallen, and the sky was dark. Below, cars still surged through the streets and the neon burned bright. Across the black expanse of water, only shown by the lack of lights, the towers of Hong Kong Island had started to darken.

There must be someone in this city who can help me, Isobel thought, tracing the light of a ferry moving across the dark water. She knew she probably didn't deserve it, but she needed it, now more than ever.

Chapter 50

The following morning, Leo woke with the taste of the evening on his tongue. They had drunk a lot. Getting out of bed, the room dancing in front of his eyes, he moved carefully to the bathroom.

Allissa was still asleep, curled up against the wall, her hair fanned out on the pillow behind.

Looking at himself in the mirror, Leo remembered – they'd solved the case. Well, Allissa wanted to get involved in a load more things, but they'd done what they set out to do. They were finished.

As Leo stood in the tiny bathroom his feeling of claustrophobia rose. The walls swayed as they moved in, cutting out the air. He drew a deep breath slowly, steadying himself on the sink. He would need to get out of this small room, get some fresh air. That would help him feel normal again. That had always been his cure for a hangover. To get out and do something, see something, try to forget about all the beer. After using the shower and dressing, he shook Allissa gently by the shoulder until her eyes fluttered open.

"I'm going out for a walk," he said. "Think I'll head up to The Peak if it's a nice day, do you wanna come?"

"Are you taking the piss?" Allissa rolled back over towards

the wall. "Walk up a giant hill. You mad?"

Before Leo shut the door, she was asleep again.

Allissa was not a morning person. For the few months Leo had known her, he didn't think she'd ever been up before ten. He was envious of her skill, he couldn't sleep beyond seven.

Outside on the balcony, the vertical village was alive with the sounds and smells of washing, cooking and children playing. Although the padlock and chain still secured the apartment next door, peace had seemed to return. Leo hoped it would stay that way.

Leo was surprised to see that Nathan Road was as busy as it always was, despite the early hour. Knowing that he couldn't face social interaction yet, Leo kept his eyes on the ground and shuffled around any bright-eyed hawkers.

The day so far was misty, the sky a dull congealed grey but Leo was sure it would clear soon.

Pushing into Tsui Tsam Tui metro station, Leo headed for the platform towards Hong Kong Island. He planned to get the train across the channel and then walk up towards The Peak. He knew it would take a while, but the exercise would do him good. He needed to clear his head after the events of the last few days.

After an hour of walking, Leo was drenched by the mist and his own efforts. The walk was arduous as the road twisted and wound around residential towers which clung precariously to the increasing slope. The surrounding towers were just phantoms in the haze and the path was just a single-track meandering beneath trees. Leo felt as though he could have been a thousand miles from the city's busy streets. The sky was still invisible beneath the fog, which hung thick and dirty.

Ahead, the road straightened out and a bridge cut across

it at an unusual incline, heading directly up the mountain. Proceeded by a rumble, Leo saw the peak train slide upwards across the bridge. Inside, the colourful clothes of its passengers smudged against the steamy glass. Looking to the right, up the incline, Leo saw the train fade into the mist. Beyond, he thought he could see the faint outline of the station, only a few hundred metres further.

Leo pushed on, climbing the steep path which followed the track. After a couple of minutes he heard the cables, which ran down the middle of the widely spaced rails, ping and crack. Then a dark shape materialized from the grey and the train shot past again, this time returning passengers back to the city.

Ahead the path opened out. To the right, the famous view of the city Leo had seen so often should have appeared. But today it was nothing but grey. In front, a few buildings surrounded a small plaza. One was the newly built train station and viewing platform, the other an entrance to a shopping mall.

Tourists milled about, taking pictures of each other – pointless without the desired backdrop.

Leo bought a bottle of water and leaned back on a bench, resting his legs. He had hoped the mist would clear while he was walking, but the thick covering of grey remained absolute.

As though coming out of the mist of his own memory, a thought suddenly occurred to Leo.

This is where the picture of Mya would have been taken.

Sitting up straight, he looked left and right.

Here somewhere.

Pulling the phone from a pocket, he scrolled through to find it. He'd kept the picture as it was the most recent one of Mya he had. In it, she stood with people he didn't recognise, the

161

city in the background.

This is where it was taken though, he thought, looking up from his phone.

But when? There was no telling. It could have been years ago. Was she still here?

To Leo, it was as though Mya represented everything that was unknown, everything that couldn't be discovered or found out. The fact that she had left, or was made to leave with no explanation, was the thing that now haunted him. Not the fact that she was gone, but the fact he didn't know. The pain of losing her had faded, but the sense of failure for not finding her grew every day.

Returning from Kathmandu with Allissa, people had assumed that this was a new start for him, that he was finally over Mya. Sometimes he'd let people think that as it was easier. But it wasn't like that.

Over the last few months Leo had encouraged Allissa to look for someone, but she never seemed interested. Part of him wanted her to for her own happiness. He knew that she had virtually always been on her own. She'd never really given being with someone a chance. But now she was more settled, it might make her happy to try. Part of him though, wanted her to be with someone because that would give him boundaries. He wouldn't have to think about her while he was lying alone in the next room. He could give up thinking about how things could be different if they were together. If Allissa was with someone else, it would make things certain and simple. Leo and Allissa were friends. That's the way he had to think about it. That's the way it was.

They been through too much together now to be anything more.

Looking back at the photo on the screen of the phone, Leo felt guilt grow in his stomach. Why had he never told Allissa about the picture? Never told her how it had been sent by her father with the promise of more information in exchange for Allissa's location.

Leo had made the decision instantly. He deleted the message, blocked and deleted Stockwell's number and would never tell Allissa about it.

But why hadn't he said anything at the time? Before it became a big issue?

When they were away, she seemed so happy. He couldn't spoil that. Then when they returned to Brighton Allissa had her dad's trial to deal with. There never seemed to be the time to tell her about the picture. He could never find the right words or the right moment.

Checking the time on his phone, Leo stood. He should head back. He wanted to get their return flights booked today. Get back as soon as possible in case he was needed at home.

Turning towards the descending path, Leo heard the people behind him start to mutter. Then as he looked out across the city, he noticed that the view had begun to change. The blue of the morning sky was appearing high up and the mist was sinking across the ocean. Leo held onto the railing in the same place Mya had stood and watched the city climb out of the fog.

At first it was just blue sky with bright sunlight crowning a thick soup of fog. Then the spires of the tallest buildings began to pierce the grey swirling mass. Within a few minutes, thirty or so buildings looked as though they were floating on a sumptuous cushion of it.

Leo turned to make his journey down the hill. With the

gleaming city came a clear mind – he was going to tell Allissa about the picture.

Chapter 51

The windows of Yee's office, where an hour ago the fog swirled like a dirty rag against the glass, were now clear. The buildings around him gleamed and in the distance the column of sea was becoming visible. It was going to turn out to be a good day.

Seated at his desk, drinking his coffee, Yee congratulated himself on a successful twenty-four hours. He'd turned what could have been a bad thing into something very good, very good indeed. Although he hadn't had the time to do what he'd wanted last night, his wife and children had now gone to visit family in Shenzen for a few days. He would have no distractions. He could do whatever he desired. Yee smiled at the thought, clenching his fists with growing excitement.

Taking another sip of the dark, bitter coffee, Yee smiled to himself. It really had worked out alright. How long it would last, he didn't know. But right now, things were going his way.

His phone vibrated on the tabletop, an unrecognised number.

"Hello," Yee answered, putting the coffee down.

"Mr Yee, it's Allissa, we met yesterday regarding your employee, Jamie Price..."

Yee grumbled. Then reminding himself Allissa knew things

165

that could damage his business, he forced a friendly tone into his voice.

"Allissa, how can I help you?"

"I'd like to know how your conversation went with Isobel – what did she say?"

"We spoke yesterday, and she no longer works at the company."

"How did she take the news? I just want to check that she's okay. Isobel may have done a bad thing, but I don't think she's necessarily a bad person. She could be vulnerable at the moment..." Yee's mind ran through the events of the past day. She certainly was vulnerable – he liked that.

"She was fine," he said. "She was a little... shocked and then she left. Took all her stuff – I'm not sure where."

The line went quiet. Yee sipped the coffee; it had gone cold.

"I'd like to speak to her," Allissa said. "I want her number please."

"Why?" Yee asked.

"I don't like loose ends with our cases, and I don't like the idea that this vulnerable young lady has no one to turn to in this city. I'd like to speak to her and check that she's alright. Can I remind you that we've done you a sizable favour coming to you first with this? It still wouldn't be too late for us to get some media interest in the story, particularly when people start asking why Jamie has been released."

Yee brooded over the answer, but he knew he didn't really have an option. Or did he...?

"Fine, I'll give it to you now," he said, the grin forming again.

Removing the phone from his ear, he scrolled through his contact list. Finding Jiao's number, he dictated it to Allissa. Jiao was with Isobel, and he could tell her exactly what to say.

"Thanks," Allissa said when she had confirmed each digit. Yee mumbled a goodbye and disconnected the call.

Yee didn't like being threatened. He wanted to be in control.

He needed to do something that would make the nosy detectives give up and go home. Then he could do whatever he wanted with Isobel. But, they couldn't think it was him doing it. If they thought he was trying to make them leave they'd become more persistent.

Leaning back on his chair, Yee examined the painting. He needed to restore order, order in which he was in control. Ruffling his fingers through the sides of his hair, Yee considered his options. He could get his way, he just had to be clever about it. Something to scare them off. Something to make them lose interest without realising it was him.

Sitting forward again he picked up his phone and called Jiao.

The idea was simple, but executed right, it might work.

Chapter 52

It takes a lot to make good coffee. It's not as easy as many people think. First the beans need to be good quality – you'd notice straight away if they weren't. They need to be kept at the right temperature and ground just before serving. The machines that steam and hiss must be cleaned and serviced regularly, and the milk (if used) must be cold and fresh. Only when these three elements are brought together will the coffee produced be rich, flavoursome, and just what Allissa needed as she walked through the door of the Serendipity Café.

She'd woken an hour earlier in a tangle of hair, fragmented memories and the insipid smell of alcohol. Leo wasn't there; she remembered him leaving some hours before, saying something mad about going for a walk.

Last night had been fun – Allissa and Leo had not been out together in a long time. They worked hard, and although it was enjoyable, they needed time off too.

Sitting at a table in the corner of the small café, Allissa thought about how things had worked out. She'd never planned anything in her life, and there had been patches of true chaos, but in the last few months she'd felt more settled than she had in a long time.

When Leo asked if she'd like to come and stay with him in Brighton for a while, Allissa wasn't sure. She'd become used to travelling, to moving on, to not staying still for long. She had tried to make something of a home in Kathmandu, but when her father ruined that, she hadn't immediately felt like trying again. But in Pokhara, spending the days enjoying the crystal lakes and the nights in city's bars and restaurants, Allissa relaxed into Leo's company.

Arriving in Brighton she had, genuinely, only intended to stay for a few weeks. But Leo's company was good, the business picked up and before she knew it, months had passed.

Allissa wasn't sure if she'd expected something to happen between them, but when it didn't, she was neither surprised nor upset. She knew the story of Mya. Leo had explained on the day they'd met. Allissa knew that part of him was still holding out for her and she wasn't going to get in the way of that.

They had become close though. Closer than she'd been with anyone in a long time.

Being honest with herself, Allissa probably didn't even know what it was like to be with anyone anyway. There had been a succession of boyfriends when she was younger, but there had been no real connections. Then, after finding out the truth about her dad, boyfriends and romance didn't really seem very important. She just wanted to go where she liked and do what made her happy without having to worry about someone else coming too.

Spending time with Leo was different though. They got on well. But not in *that* way.

Then when she'd been in Brighton a few weeks, for the second time in her life, everything changed. The prosecution

169

of her dad. He had been charged with a series of offences including organising the murder of her mother in Kenya. The walls had closed in as she was asked to testify.

Allissa had to decide whether to stand up for her mother against her father or refuse to testify against her father and feel like she was dishonouring her mother. It was a bleak choice.

After many sleepless nights of indecision, Allissa decided that if she told the story – told the truth, her truth – then it was up to the court whether or not to find him guilty. She would have done her bit.

Leo held her hand that day as they left the court. She hadn't been touched like that in a long time. Tears streaked her face as they sat outside in the cold afternoon. Leo said nothing, he didn't need to. He held her tight against his shoulder until her sobbing subsided and then they made the journey home together.

They were just friends, she was sure of it. Things were great the way they were. They'd both been through so much that simple was better.

That's what Allissa told herself, her mind roaming in the corner of the café.

"Do you know what you want?" A voice punctured her daydream. "What can I get you?" A waitress stood over her, a small pad and pen in hand.

"Ah, yeah, flat white please," Allissa said, closing the menu she had laid in front of her but not even glanced at.

"Sure, I'll sort that for you now," the waitress said with a smile.

Something about her surprised Allissa, her English accent to start with.

Allissa watched her crossing the empty café. She was pretty, tall, slender, large wide eyes and a broad smile that lit her face with warmth. *Strange*, Allissa thought, dismissing it as her phone vibrated.

It was a message from Leo: *Hey. On my way back now, see you in a bit. x*

Allissa dismissed the message as the coffee machine began to hiss and steam industriously. Allissa watched the girl operate it. She did look sort of familiar, but Allissa just couldn't place her.

Maybe they'd seen her out the previous night, or she looked like a famous person.

Bloody hangover déjà vu, Allissa thought picking up her phone again. If she wanted to talk to Isobel, she should do it before Leo came back.

Allissa knew what it was like to be afraid with no one to turn to. So, despite Leo's assertion that the job was finished, Allissa knew she had to at least check that Isobel was alright. She dialled the number Yee had given her as the waitress brought the coffee. She smiled in thanks.

"Hello?"

"Is that Isobel?"

"Yes, who's this?"

Allissa explained who she was and how she and Leo had been paid by Jamie to prove his innocence. Isobel seemed to be listening intently.

"I just wanted to check that you're okay, whatever you've done, I'm sure you had your reasons. I couldn't just leave you."

Allissa paused expecting a torrent of abuse. None came.

"Can you meet me?" Isobel said.

"Yeah, of course," Allissa said, in surprise. "Where?"

"There's a restaurant on Cameron Road. The Golden Lotus," Isobel said without seeming to think about it. "Come at two."

Chapter 53

The metro from Hong Kong Island back to Kowloon hummed as it accelerated out of the station. In contrast to the morning's crossing, the train was almost empty. Sitting down, Leo felt his phone vibrate. *Strange.* He was used to London's underground system which no phone signals could permeate. Pulling it from his pocket he saw Allissa's name flashing on the screen. Looking left and right, as though observing a private miracle, he answered.

"Hey, I'm on the metro coming back from The Peak – how you feeling?" Leo didn't even need to raise his voice against the electric murmur of the train.

"Yeah getting there, coffee is helping," Allissa said. "Isobel just called, she wants to meet us. Just to explain stuff, I think."

Leo felt his frustration build. This wasn't how it was supposed to go.

"I thought we agreed last night that we would just call to check she's okay. Not meet her for lunch."

"I know, I called her, and she suggested it. I'm worried about her."

Leo didn't reply as the metro began to slow.

"I know you didn't want to get involved," Allissa said, "but she's alone and she's vulnerable."

"Okay, where?" Leo said. He knew Allissa wouldn't give up; it would be better to just go and get it done.

Leo's journey from the metro station was quick in the dwindling lunchtime crowd.

Although shoppers, tourists and salesmen still meandered and hassled across the wide pavements, Leo avoided them decisively. A few minutes later, he waited where Allissa had told him – on the corner of Nathan Road and Cameron Road. He was early.

As a procession of taxis queued to turn, Leo shivered, his body cooling after the day's exertion. The sky was a thick blue in the now-bright afternoon.

From the wide, sun-lit pavement of Nathan Road, Cameron Road looked dark. It was thin and lay in the constant shadow of the looming buildings either side.

Squinting down the dismal street, trying to make out The Golden Lotus where Isobel had asked to meet, Leo was reminded of the restaurant they'd visited in Kathmandu. That wasn't a visit he or Allissa would want to relive, or ever forget. It may have been the memory, or his cooling body temperature, but Leo felt himself shudder.

After five minutes, Allissa arrived from the other direction. Seeing her emerge from the crowd, Leo found himself smiling. As she smiled back, he remembered he was supposed to be irritated with the whole situation.

"All Isobel said was that she wanted to meet us here?" Leo said by way of greeting.

"Pretty much, yeah."

"Sounds a bit strange to me."

"I imagine she just wants someone to talk to – to get things straight. She sounded really timid on the phone."

Leo rubbed a hand across his chin and hummed doubtfully.

"Look, it's not going to make any difference. We will go now, see what she has to say, check she's alright and then we will be done. Then this afternoon we will go and get our flights home booked."

Leo felt himself warming at the suggestion as he followed Allissa into the shadows of Cameron Road.

"How are you feeling anyway?" He asked.

Allissa exhaled. "Better than I was an hour ago. Last night was fun though."

"Yes, it was," Leo agreed.

Cameron Road became increasingly gloomy the further they walked. Above, only a slither of sky was visible between the dirty shadows of the buildings. It seemed that the road only existed to serve the goods entrances to the shops either side.

"Is that it?" Leo said, pointing to a bunch of discoloured letters above what looked like a disused restaurant on the right-hand side. Some of the letters were covered in grime and others were missing entirely.

"Must be," Allissa said.

"You sure this is the place?"

Leo crossed the road to get a closer look. He peered in through the filthy window on which a faded menu still clung, the tape that held it yellowed with age. Inside, dust lay across red plastic tables and chairs.

"It doesn't look open."

"The Golden Lotus, Cameron Road." Allissa checked the name of the street on her phone to make sure. "That's what she said. This is it."

An air-conditioner on the wall above them rattled to life.

"What time is it now?" Leo asked.

"Five past."

"Alright, we will give her five minutes. I'm not wasting our time playing games."

Allissa nodded before peering through the window.

"I'm not eating here either," Leo said.

"I don't think there'll be anything on the menu you'll like," Allissa replied. "It's a shame, I was looking forward to lunch."

Allissa cupped her hands above her eyes in an attempt to get a better view of the inside.

"It doesn't look like it's been open in years," she said, before crossing to the door.

Trying the handle, the door swung open.

Looking back at Leo, she shrugged.

"Hello?" Allissa shouted through the open door, her voice echoing in the empty room.

There was no reply.

"Hello...?" she shouted again and stepped into the restaurant.

"Don't..." Leo said, grabbing her by the arm. "It might..."

"Oh, come on," Allissa said, pulling her arm away. Leo noticed a spark of excitement in her eyes. "We'll just have a look around, then we'll go."

As Leo looked up at the place, a bad feeling started to bubble in his stomach. He folded his arms tight across his chest.

"We really should just wait out here for her," he shouted to Allissa who was already inside.

She didn't answer.

"Allissa," Leo shouted again. "I've got a bad feeling about this. It's just..."

Exhaling aggressively, Leo let his arms drop. He knew he

couldn't let Allissa go in there alone.

Looking left and right along the road, Leo tried to ignore the fear which had now risen to his chest. Then taking a deep breath, he followed Allissa into the restaurant.

Chapter 54

Yee had said it would be simple, that no one would get hurt, that it was just to scare them off. Even so, cowering in a passage next to The Golden Lotus restaurant, Isobel felt a sickening feeling rise in her stomach. These people had ruined her plans, but she didn't want them to get hurt.

Next to her, Jiao knelt down and opened the valve on the restaurant's gas supply.

Isobel knew what he was doing, she'd seen him tear the gas feed from the stove and set up a detonation device in the kitchen.

"It's not going to kill them," Jiao reassured her. "It's set on a delay."

Isobel tried to swallow but her throat was dry.

"Opening the back door is the trigger," Jiao said, pointing towards the kitchen door at the back of the restaurant. "As long as they get out quickly, they'll be fine."

"Is this it?" came a voice from the street. Another replied.

The passage was concealed from the street by a thin metal door, from behind which Isobel and Jiao listened. Jiao held a thick finger to his lips and began to smile.

First, Leo and Allissa discussed the restaurant while they

waited outside. It took them a couple of minutes to try the door.

Realising it was open, as Yee said they would, Allissa walked inside. A few seconds later, Leo followed.

Isobel swallowed hard and tried to ignore the thudding of her heart. Jiao pulled a key from the inside pocket of his jacket.

"All you have to do is lock them in, so they have to leave through the back," he whispered handing Isobel the key. "And make sure they see it's you."

Chapter 55

"Be careful," Leo grumbled as he followed Allissa into the restaurant.

"Hello?" Allissa shouted again, her voice sounding loud in the empty room. She thought she could hear movement somewhere, perhaps out the back.

The restaurant smelled of decay, dust and stale air. A dozen plastic tables stood empty, faded murals of rural China covered the walls.

A noise from somewhere in the building, the kitchen maybe.

"Anyone here? Isobel?" Allissa shouted again.

Silence, no reply.

She turned to look at Leo.

"Doesn't look like she's here," Leo said, looking around the empty room. Behind them, now a few steps away, the door remained open.

A noise again, something closing, slamming. Both looked towards the kitchen.

"Hello? Anyone?" Leo shouted.

Nothing.

"Let's have a look around," Allissa said, "then we'll get out of here."

In the kitchen, pots and pans lay next to a large stove with six blackened rings. An extractor fan on the wall tapped in the wind and a stained steel sink sat next to a door leading out the back. The place was empty.

"There's no one here," Leo said standing at the door.

"But why would she want us –"

There was a thud from the front of the restaurant. A door slammed. A key grated in the lock. Both turned to see the door shuddering against its frame. Through the glass panel of the door, they saw, checking it was properly secured, Isobel.

"What are you doing?" Leo shouted as they watched her try the handle. Her long red hair was tied back. Her eyes seemed vacant and puffy.

"Hello!" Leo shouted again, crossing the room.

Isobel didn't look up, with a morose expression she turned and walked away.

"What was the point of that?" Leo said, turning to look at Allissa. "This has been such a waste of time, playing her games."

Leo pulled on the door. Nothing moved. It was solid. He tried again. The lock held – if anything he was going to pull the handle from the wooden frame.

"Bitch," Leo said, trying the door again. "What is this girl playing at? This is why we don't get involved."

Pushing the door in anger, Leo turned to Allissa.

"I mean, what is the point?" Leo strode across the restaurant and back into the kitchen. "Hold on. Can you smell that?"

The smell was faint.

Allissa stopped moving and sniffed the air. "Yeah, what is it?"

"Not sure."

Leo looked around the room, he'd seen the cooker, stained

with years of hot, fizzing oil. Then he noticed a gap where it had been pulled from the wall. Leaning over, he looked down the back, six inches or so between the wall of the kitchen and the steel of the appliance.

The hose hissed gently, filling the room.

"Gas," he shouted across to Allissa. "It's gas – that smell. We need to get out of here now."

Chapter 56

At the end of the street Jiao stopped and turned to face the restaurant.

"We wait to check it's done," he said, letting go of Isobel's arm. Her skin stung where his fingers had dragged her away.

Around them, traffic surged in both directions. A taxi pulled in and three tourists got out, their eyes transfixed on the towers which surrounded them. They were free, like Isobel had been just days ago.

She could run. Try her luck, head to the embassy, the police, anywhere. It wouldn't matter as long as it was away from Jiao and away from Yee. The thought of Yee made her throat sting.

She had no money, no passport, but anything would be better than facing him again.

"You can try to run," Yee had told her before leaving the previous afternoon. "I'll call my friends in the police, they'll pick you up at the airport. They'll stop flights leaving if needed. You don't build a city like this," he said stepping closer and trying to catch her eye, "without making influential friends. I've done deals with every important person in this city. Some of them honest, some of them not."

But could he really do that? Was anyone really that important?

It might be worth a try.

Next to her, Jiao stared at the restaurant. Watching for any sign of the explosion.

A bus nudged its way towards them through the traffic. If she got on, would Jiao risk making a scene by pulling her off? Was the risk worth it?

Isobel thought of Yee's smile, the cold touch of his fingers, the smell of drink on his breath. She couldn't go back.

Looking at Jiao, the mask of a smile fixed to his face as he watched expectantly, Isobel made a decision.

It may take him a second to notice that she'd gone. Hopefully a second was enough.

Chapter 57

The smell of gas which had at first given a sweet chemical zing to the air now lay heavy and thick. The broken pipe behind the cooker continued to hiss as gas filled the kitchen and streamed out into the restaurant.

"This wasn't an accident," Leo said, peering down behind the stove. "Someone's cut it."

"Isobel?" Allissa questioned. "But why would she want to do this?"

"Well, we've sort of messed her life up," Leo held the pipe trying to reduce the flow of gas. His knuckles whitened with the pressure. "We need to get out of here now," he looked at Allissa, "this could catch at any time."

Allissa tried the handle of the front door again – locked solid. The glass of the front window would be thick; commercial windows were designed to be difficult to break for security reasons.

"Try that door," Leo shouted, pointing with his free hand to the door which led out the back. "It's probably locked, but worth a try.

Through the door's dirty, barred window, Leo could see bins, rotting storage boxes and a pair of broken chairs in the small yard. He could taste the gas now, it was clawing, choking, clogging his throat and nose. He started to cough.

Between his fingers, Leo felt it run as his grip weakened.

He couldn't stop coughing.

Reaching the door, Allissa held her breath as she tried the handle.

All Leo heard was his own raspy coughs and the peaceful hiss of the noxious gas.

The handle moved.

Allissa pulled open the door.

"Out, now," Allissa shouted. "Go."

Rushing through the door, neither noticed the device which Jiao had set begin its countdown. It was a simple thing. Just a large remote-controlled cigarette lighter from which a flame would appear at a particular moment. Normally harmless. But in a room full of flammable gas, explosive.

Chapter 58

Jiao knew that from a distance an explosion appears to be one complete sound. It's only when you get up close that it breaks down like the players in an orchestra. To begin with there's the high whining sounds, increasing in pitch as flames start to rip. Then the sound of the windows shattering. Then the thump and flutter as oxygen is dragged in by the hungry fire.

Neither Leo nor Allissa expected the explosion as they stumbled out into the street. Each taking deep, greedy breaths.

Leo was forced to the floor and Allissa against the wall of the opposite building. But they were out, and they were alive.

Allissa leaned on the wall as her breathing calmed. Leo stood hunched, hands on his knees and spat the taste of fire and gas from his mouth.

"That girl has some serious issues," Leo said, wiping his hand across his mouth and straightening up. "How did she…"

"I just don't know." Allissa said, coughing.

"That girl," Leo pointed back at the restaurant, his hands blackened, "the girl you were so bothered about, just tried to kill us."

"But why?"

Leo took a deep breath and spat the taste of fire again.

Allissa stood, straightening her back. She had an ache in her thigh. She must have bashed it during the escape.

Thoughts crowded her mind like the smoke which now poured into the sky. How had she got it so wrong? Had she let the vulnerable women she used to protect cloud her judgement? Allissa knew her mistake had almost killed them both.

"I'm sorry," she said, stepping across to Leo. "I could have got us killed. I just saw something in her that needed help."

Leo took a deep breath, letting the last bit of his frustration go.

Across the road the fire still burned.

"It's fine, it's fine," he said, looking at Allissa who stood next to him.

Without warning, Allissa hugged him. Pulled her body close to his. Leo stood rigid in shock until he realised what was happening, then put his arms around her.

"But if she's done this to us, what's she going to do to Yee?" Allissa said, breaking from the embrace and stepping backwards. "I hope his family aren't at home."

Leo said nothing.

"She'll be going there," Allissa said. "She must be angry at people for messing with her plans. She'll want revenge against him too, I'm sure."

From the grind of the city and the rumble of the fire, sirens became audible. Allissa looked towards the sound.

"I suppose you're going to say we need to stay here, wait for the fire brigade and that what happens with Isobel, Yee and his family is not our problem?" Allissa said, brushing herself down.

Leo tried to think but his mind was still clogged with

adrenaline of the fire and the intimacy of their embrace. As his thoughts cleared, Leo realized they hadn't asked for this. Isobel had brought this on them. They'd done their job and now she'd dragged them back in. Then he thought about how nice it felt to hold Allissa close and how, in reality, he would do anything for her.

"Hell no," Leo said, brushing the soot off himself as the first fire engine rounded the corner, blue lights strobing. "Yee has a family, and there's no telling what Isobel will do." Leo said, running in the opposite direction. "We're involved now."

Chapter 59

"With the new evidence presented, you can't seriously be continuing to charge my client with murder?" Jamie's lawyer berated the judge, pacing up and down the courtroom. It was an emergency hearing, called on the back of the revealing new evidence received yesterday. Photos of Isobel, alive. One of these photos, Isobel walking into an office building, was being displayed on a large screen.

"This could have been taken at any time," the judge said, taking off his glasses and leaning forwards.

The lawyer flicked to the next image – Isobel in the reception area of OZ Architecture. The time and date was stamped clearly in the top right-hand corner.

"As you can see, Isobel is alive and well and living in Hong Kong," the lawyer said, standing still for a moment to add gravity to his next statement. "She is the one who should be charged as she has taken the identity of my client in order to claim the salary of his job. We have a written statement from the company."

"How do we know these pictures are real, your honour?" came a voice from elsewhere in the room.

"I've had the court's expert look over them," the lawyer

replied. "They show no signs of being tampered with – you have his report in front of you. May I read this statement, your honour?"

The judge nodded. The lawyer read the statement, loud and slow, pausing before the final sentence.

"This bit is particularly interesting," he said, looking at the judge. "We have had no reason to doubt *her*" – the lawyer paused allowing the importance of the pronoun to sink in – "honesty, but since learning of these claims she has been dismissed."

"In the light of this evidence," the judge said, clearing his throat, "a murder charge is inappropriate. It's clear the young lady is still alive. Mr Price, you are free to go."

With the words "free to go," months of tension flowed from Jamie's body. He was free. It was over.

After all those nights of captivity, shadows and sleeplessness, he was free.

He'd not felt the sun on his face, not seen his friends, nor really seen his family other than across the metal table of the visiting room for one hour a week.

An hour later, he walked from court and looked up at the sky. When he'd gone inside the sky had been grey and dreary. The pastel wash of a new year. Now a harsh blue curved above him, smelling and tasting like spring.

"Those guys did a great job finding her," Jamie's brother said from beside him, crossing to a waiting taxi.

"What? Ah, yeah, they did," Jamie replied in a daze, following him into the car. "They've pretty much saved my life. I'd better send them the money."

Chapter 60

Isobel knew she had a second, maybe less, to put some distance between herself and Jiao's impenetrable grip. Looking at Jiao as the explosion sounded, his eyes widening greedily at the fire, she knew this was her time. She darted for a group of tourists, gawping at the window display of a designer shop.

As the group scattered, Isobel expected at any moment to feel Jiao's fingers around her shoulder or neck, but it didn't come.

Not daring to look back, she sprinted on, pushing pedestrians to the left and right, her flat shoes making easy work of the pavement. Jiao wouldn't be far behind. She needed to get as far away as quickly as possible. Ideally out of Hong Kong.

Pushing herself up Nathan Road, darting left and right through the crowds, Isobel started to formulate a plan.

She needed to get away from Yee, his henchmen and everything he owned or controlled. But how? She had her passport and some money in her hotel room. Yee and Jiao didn't know anything about that, did they?

Looking at the traffic, growling past at a pace slower than she was running, Isobel had a thought. The hotel was only three streets away. If she ran all the way, she could get back there quicker than Jiao would by car, even if he knew where he was going.

She could get in, grab her passport and money, and be out by the time he arrived. It was daring and dangerous, as it was the obvious place to go. But if she was quick enough, she could be out with everything she needed before they caught up. There would be seconds to spare. It felt like her only option.

Turning right into a quiet backstreet, Isobel accelerated. Every second counted. Even meeting Jiao on the way out would mean failure. Get in, get her stuff, get out.

She would leave her clothes, leave her bag, she didn't need them. Just the folder containing her passport, a bit of cash and an emergency credit card.

As her trainers pounded the pavement and her breathing started to regulate to the speed of the run, Isobel thought about where exactly the folder was. She pictured it, about the size of a diary, made of pink fabric, hidden behind the dressing table.

She remembered putting it there thinking that if the sleazy hotel owner, or anyone else, went in her room they wouldn't see it. They could rifle through her drawers, but her essential documents would stay safe.

She took the next corner at speed, charging out onto a main road. Beside her four lanes of traffic inched forward. Jiao would be on the way now, Isobel knew it. The thought of his grin and the touch of Yee's hand made her push faster. Her muscles stung.

She was close; one more turn and she was there. She just wanted to get out. Get home.

Springing across the road, dodging the cars which nudged forward bumper to bumper, Isobel's breathing burned with petrol fumes. She ran into the backstreet her hotel occupied. The shadow of the building cast a chill across her skin.

There was no sign that Jiao was there yet. Yee's car wasn't outside.

Stopping at the door, her feet sliding on the dirty concrete, she slammed her palm on to the door entry buzzer.

Come on. Come on...

"Shi." The hotelier's voice sounded distant on the small speaker.

Wrenching the door open when it buzzed, Isobel took the stairs two at a time.

At the top the hotelier sat, as he always did, behind the small reception desk. He was eating noodles from a box, the sauce dribbling down his chin and onto his shirt.

"Hi," Isobel said, trying to control her frantic breathing. "I've lost my key, can you let me in please?"

He frowned, not hiding his eyes travelling across her body.

"I'd be so grateful," Isobel said, forcing a smile.

Quickly! I need to go!

With an effort, he lifted his bulk from behind the small reception desk and pushed past Isobel. Her smile dropped as soon as he was in front of her.

Stopping outside the door of Isobel's room, he took a bunch of keys from his pocket.

Sorting through them took an age.

Selecting one, he slid it into the lock.

Isobel readied herself to leap forwards as the lock disengaged. It didn't. The key didn't move.

With a grumble the hotelier removed it again.

Isobel's eyes darted from the hotelier who searched again through the dozen or so keys to the phone on the reception desk. She imagined Jiao pulling up outside. The black car bumping up on to the kerb. Jiao getting out, straightening his suit as he pressed the door entry buzzer.

Selecting another key, the hotelier examined it closely, holding it up between thick greasy fingers. Then slid it forcefully into the lock, this time it opened.

"Thank you, thank you." Isobel pushed past him into the room.

The folder was behind the dressing table, she was sure of it. Without even switching on the light she crossed the room. Taking a deep breath, she pulled the dressing table away from the wall.

There was no time. She needed to get out. She could not go back there. Not tonight.

Peering down behind the dressing table, Isobel's heart sunk. The space was empty. It wasn't there. She must have put it somewhere else.

Frantically she started to check. Where was it? She searched the drawers, the bottom of her bag, beneath the bed. She was rummaging through one of the bedside tables when a figure moved across the doorway. It was just a silhouette against the rectangle of light from the hallway, but as Isobel turned, she could see in their hand a small pink folder.

"Are you looking for something?" came Jiao's unmistakable voice.

Chapter 61

The lights of Hong Kong's mid-levels began to strain to life as the sun started its descent through oily strips of cloud.

"But how do you know where he lives?" Leo said, following Allissa from the metro station and into the mild air.

"Do you remember yesterday, you read his profile online?"

"Yes." Leo pulled out his phone and reloaded the page.

"It said he lived in the Hong Kong mid-levels area," Allissa said.

"Yeah, but there are loads of residential towers there."

"Yes," Allissa said, stopping to face Leo. "But then it said he won an award for one he designed last year."

Leo nodded as he read it again on the screen.

"Can you really see Yee living in someone else's building?"

Leo smiled with affection. Allissa always impressed him.

"No, of course not. He would have to live in his own tower," Leo said. Maybe it was just that he was impressed. She was a very impressive person.

Allissa turned and began to walk.

"There's no point getting a taxi," Allissa shouted back over her shoulder. "Too much traffic. If we walk quickly, we'll be there in twenty minutes."

"What do you think Isobel is going to do?" Leo asked as they crossed between stationary cars.

"I don't know, but she must have been properly pissed off to do that to us," Allissa said, watching the pulsing blue dot on the screen. "She's obviously pretty capable – that wouldn't have been an easy thing to do."

The pair stopped to allow a tram to rattle past.

"I just hope Yee's family aren't home, for their safety," Allissa said, pointing in the direction they needed to go.

"Yeah, well, she'll only be a few minutes ahead of us. We need to warn him. Try to call again."

They had tried before but there was no answer; the phone rang out.

They crossed another road in the shadow of a towering apartment building. Along the length of the street, stalls selling fish and seafood began to pack their stock back into boxes of ice for the end of the day. Leo noticed the strange looks they were receiving, dirty and bedraggled in the gleaming city.

"Ten minutes away," Allissa said, checking the screen. The road had started to steepen as the walk became more difficult. Lights rippled on in buildings above. Leo noticed that Allissa was limping, although she hadn't slowed despite the pain.

His own legs felt heavy after the climb this morning. He remembered what he wanted to tell her, about Stockwell's picture of Mya. That would wait until later.

"Come on, keep up," Allissa turned and shouted back at him as they approached a flight of stairs. He saw a glint in her eye brought on by the adrenaline. "We've got to stop this mad woman."

197

Chapter 62

"I don't understand, how did you...?" Isobel asked as Jiao closed in on her in the small room.

"We must hurry, we're already late with this running around. Mr Yee wanted you at his apartment half an hour ago."

"No, I'm not..."

"Yes, you are." Jiao grabbed her wrist, twisted it so Isobel had to walk on tiptoes, then led her from the room and out into the corridor.

"Help me," she implored the hotelier, whose eyes darted from the television to Isobel hopping in pain. "Call the police, I'm..."

"Thank you," said Jiao, speaking in English, doubtless so Isobel could understand. Without letting go of Isobel, he handed over a small wad of notes. The hotelier reached out for them whilst stuffing another tangle of noodles in his mouth.

"You think we hadn't thought you might do that?" Jiao said, forcing Isobel down the stairs one at a time.

Chapter 63

From the 28th floor, Yee's apartment had a commanding view of the city. It clung to the slope against The Peak's steep incline. Yee loved looking down on the other buildings, it gave him the impression that he was on top of the world. Which, he supposed, taking another sip of whiskey, he was.

In Yee's line of work a lot of people were out to bring him down, to cheat him, to make him seem like an idiot. He always dealt with them one way – harshly.

As Yee watched the darkening office towers of lower Hong Kong from his balcony, a cold, clear breeze rolled in from the sea. Yee was looking forward to tonight. He was dealing with someone who had tried to deceive him, and he was going to enjoy it. It felt like he had been waiting days for this. Tonight, he would finally get to spend some time with Isobel. They'd be alone and uninterrupted. *That body* – he bristled with the thought. He'd have all the time he wanted. The whole night. To do anything he wanted.

Taking a sip of the whiskey, Yee bit his lower lip in anticipation. He had wanted this ever since he first saw her walk into his office. The kiss had made his blood rush with desire and excitement. But it wasn't until he'd learned of her deceit that he knew he could make it happen. He could make her his.

Hearing the doorbell, Yee put his glass down next to the half-empty bottle.

As he walked into the living room, the lights sprung on automatically, glinting from the marble floor tiles and white walls adorned in modern art and Chinese artefacts. This was his room. The children were forbidden from playing in here.

Crossing the space, Yee straightened his jacket and opened the door. Excitement welled through him.

In the hallway, Isobel stood with Jiao behind her. She looked sulky and forlorn.

"Is it done?" Yee asked Jiao, speaking in English so Isobel could understand.

"Yes," Jiao said. "They'll survive, but I doubt they'll be bothering you again. She did a good job."

Jiao shoved Isobel forwards, causing her to stumble towards Yee.

"Although we did have a little run around afterwards. She went to get this from her hotel," Jiao said, handing the folder over. Isobel's eyes followed it.

"You weren't planning to leave without saying goodbye, were you?" Yee took the folder and looked at Isobel with a raised eyebrow.

He opened it and peered inside. A passport, a few banknotes and a credit card.

"You won't need this tonight," Yee said, throwing it across the room where it landed on the leather sofa. Isobel looked at it longingly.

Putting a hand on Isobel's hip, Yee pulled her forwards. She really did look delicious. It was everything Yee had wanted. Excitement rippled across his body.

"Excellent, good work," Yee said to Jiao, switching to Cantonese. "That'll be all I need tonight. Go home and relax."

"You sure, what if…?"

"It'll be fine. I don't want to be disturbed."

Jiao nodded and turned towards the lift.

Yee closed the door and shoved Isobel further into the room. Her arms were folded and her shoulders hunched.

Yee took in her profile from behind and grinned.

"You've done really well today," he said, standing close behind her. "Maybe you deserve something good…"

Isobel didn't reply.

Yee couldn't quite believe she was finally here. All the delays. All the distractions. But now she was his.

From behind, Yee started to explore Isobel's body, moving his hands across her curves. Then he pulled her in close and kissed her neck. Isobel fought a sob as she stumbled backwards.

"Don't do anything stupid now," Yee said, as though talking to a child. "Just do what you're told, and you might even enjoy it."

He brushed her cheek with a finger and moved his mouth close to hers. "You're only going to make things worse for yourself if you don't do what you're told. I really wouldn't want you to get hurt."

Feeling Isobel's body, the image of his wife appeared in Yee's mind. The woman he'd been married to for nearly twenty years. The woman who'd been there for him and given him two children. Sure, they'd loved each other at the start. Young people don't know any better. But the long hours at the firm. The long hours which paid for this apartment, paid for the girls' school, paid for their holidays had taken their toll. There was no love anymore, and he'd grown tired of her slim, frail figure. This is what he needed, he thought, focusing his attention on Isobel's breasts.

Isobel said nothing, her body rigid, fists balled. Yee stepped back and spun her by the shoulders to face him.

Behind Isobel, the final light faded from the skyline. The inky darkness was becoming absolute.

With a welling sense of excitement, Yee decided he couldn't wait.

"Go and have a shower," he said, indicating the door which led to the master bedroom and en-suite shower. "Then put the dress on I've laid out for you and we will have a drink on the balcony."

Yee walked around her to the window. "You've got five minutes."

As Yee turned to look at the city below, Isobel's eyes ran to the door she'd just come through.

Out on the balcony, Yee refilled his glass and looked across the purring city. From inside he heard the shower start. In the dark sky a plane banked high as it lined up to land at Hong Kong International Airport. It had been a good day. Yee felt buoyant. He'd had a difficult couple of months but now things were lining up to land for him.

They were working on a couple of troublesome projects. There were two sites he already owned and wanted to re-develop. A week ago, he'd finally managed to get the permission he needed to get started on one of them. The demolition was scheduled for tomorrow.

The other was proving more difficult, but Yee knew they'd find a way. There was always a way.

He took a sip from the cooled whiskey as he thought. The

problem was it had tenants in it. It was his building, he owned the concrete and steel and glass, but the law also recognised that it was the tenants' homes. He had tried everything so far, bribing officials, threatening court action, offering to re-house the tenants. Nothing had worked. He'd spiked the rents up and evicted a few of them – the more forcefully the better. But now they had joined forces and were living together in order to continue to pay him the rent collectively. It was so frustrating.

Today, though, he had a settled on a new plan, something low-tech. The simple solutions were the best. A fire.

Jiao was good with fires. Today's trial had proven that.

Yee found the thought excited him. Maybe even more than the thought of Isobel in the shower.

A fire. Ripping through the building, the pesky tenants scuttling for their lives. Rats from a sinking ship.

With them gone, he could move in and redevelop as he pleased. He wouldn't even have to honour the promise of rehousing them. They would be on their own. A smile spread across his face with the thought. Yes, things were working out very nicely.

There was one complication though. Isobel. She would get in the way if he let her linger. He would have to get rid of her. But that didn't mean he couldn't have some fun with her first.

There was another knock at the door.

Walking back into the room, Yee heard the shower still rumbling away. Steam curled across the ceiling.

Opening the door, Yee was surprised to see Isobel, again with Jiao behind her. A red mark had started to form across her face. It took Yee a few moments to work out what had happened.

"I was just talking with the security guard downstairs," Jiao said, "and look who should come walking down. Obviously, she thought she could just leave."

Yee shook his head as he looked the woman up and down. "You'll be punished for this."

Yee pushed Isobel towards the bedroom. Jiao craned his neck to watch.

"Thanks Jiao," Yee said. "You can go now, I'll keep a close watch on her."

Yee closed the door and shoved Isobel again.

"Now get undressed and get in the shower," Yee demanded.

Isobel signalled for him to leave.

"No, you can't be trusted to be on your own now."

"No, I'm not…"

The slap silenced her.

Yee grinned with exhilaration.

"Do it now," he said. Isobel held her cheek. Yee noticed her eyes becoming watery; it looked as though she was fighting it.

She began to undress, unzipping the sports top, the strap top underneath. The removal of each brought a pang of excitement. Yee watched open-mouthed.

When she was naked, Isobel crossed the room to the shower. Yee followed her and stood at the door. He watched the beads of water fall across her body. Running over her nipples, down her back, across her bum.

He felt his breathing quicken as he thought of how good she would feel. How, even if she made a fuss, he would get what he wanted. He'd waited for this. He deserved it.

It was a shame she'd have to go.

Chapter 64

Down at street level, Allissa and Leo pushed on. Allissa's phone reported that they were now only a couple of minutes from the building. Although it didn't tell them exactly which one of the dark silhouettes was the tower they wanted.

Isobel had a fifteen-minute head start and she knew where she was going. That could make all the difference. Allissa and Leo didn't talk about what they might find when they arrived at Yee's flat. Allissa didn't think it would be good.

Walking into a small plaza surrounded by towers, Allissa looked down at the screen of her phone.

"That's it, I think," she said pointing towards a tower of green glass and orange concrete which looked over them to the left. On the screen of her phone the pin was securely planted on it.

But, crossing the plaza, the phone's pulsing blue dot changed its mind and slid across the screen. The building in front couldn't be the one they needed. If the location was correct this time, Yee's apartment was somewhere behind.

"It's the reflection from the glass," Allissa said, looking from the phone in her hand to the surrounding buildings. "It confuses the satellite signal."

Leo looked around the plaza without reply.

It was almost dark now; the sky had mellowed from a burnt and hazy orange to a deep plum. Streetlights washed Leo and Allissa with their occasional half-light, and the opulent light from the towers looked welcoming.

"Got it," Allissa said, walking forwards without waiting. Behind the first, another tower came into view. It overshadowed its neighbours in height, elevation and splendour. Blazoned on the side in bright white, *The Address.*

"This is it. This is the one Yee designed," Allissa said. She felt confident that Yee would live in his own building. But which floor or apartment, she had no idea.

Looking up at the building, Allissa felt fear twist in the stomach. It must have been over sixty stories high. More apartments were now in light than those in darkness. There was no way she could even guess how many apartments there were. Allissa ran her eyes across them. And just one of them, possibly, contained the woman they were looking for. The woman who had sent a man to prison for three months, tried to kill them and now endangered the lives of Yee and his family.

Chapter 65

The dress Yee had laid out for Isobel was tight and short. It cut aggressively beneath her breasts, pushing them upwards and squeezed her waist and legs. She walked across to the mirror in the large bedroom, finding each step a struggle. She took no pleasure in the fact she looked good. There was no pleasure in any of this. Looking good just meant he'd enjoy it more. The thought repelled her, but what choice did she have?

"Are you ready?" Yee's voice echoed from the living room. He had left the doorway to refill his drink.

As Isobel walked out into the room, Yee inhaled sharply. His eyes explored her body and his chest seemed to rise and fall with greater depth. An animalistic growl came from between his sharp, bared teeth. Yee was ready for fun.

Chapter 66

Pushing open the doors of The Address, Leo and Allissa walked into the entrance hall. Catching a glance of their reflection in the doors, Leo thought how bedraggled they looked, how out of place in the opulent foyer. For a few seconds he felt dazed by the bright overhead lights and the hush of the air conditioning.

The building made Leo think of the sort of flat his family tried to talk him into buying back in England. Sterile and characterless. Although they may be spacious, shiny and new, they were still life in a box. Life constricted and confined into a designer unit. The battery human.

Without a backwards glance, Allissa crossed to the concierge who sat behind a desk in the middle of the room. He looked up as Allissa approached. If her appearance surprised him, he didn't show it.

Leo hung back towards the lifts, leaning on his heels to look relaxed.

"Good evening," Allissa said, flashing him a smile. Leo nodded a greeting. "We're here to see Mr Yee, he knows we're coming." Allissa's confidence, as always, impressed Leo, who smiled nervously.

"I'll call up for you, madam," the concierge replied, returning her smile and picking up one of the phones on the desk in front of him. His eyes stayed on Allissa as he dialled.

Leo watched the bank of elevators. Two were making their way down and one was already on the ground floor.

The concierge held the phone to his ear for a few seconds. Leo felt his anxiety rise, a tightness in his chest. He focused on his breathing to calm it.

Breathe in and out. Focus and calm.

Silence hung over the foyer.

One of the lifts chimed and the brass doors slid open. A Chinese family wandered out. Their voices hushed as they passed Leo, the two children staring at him in interest.

"I'm afraid there's no answer," the man said, putting the phone down. "What are you here for?"

"We're doing some work for Mr Yee," Allissa said without hesitation. "It's of a private nature. He's asked us here on a matter of urgency."

"I see, head up then, he may just be busy at the moment."

"Thanks," Allissa said, her smile widening as she headed for the lifts.

"Oh, one more thing," she said. "My phone has run out of battery so I can't see the e-mail he sent me. What number is his apartment?"

The man looked quizzically at her and then across to Leo.

Leo focused on his breathing. If they couldn't get the information, finding him from floor to floor would take hours. They could be too late.

The phone on the desk started to buzz. The concierge reached to answer it.

"Floor twenty-eight. Flat three."

Chapter 67

I sobel felt her body tense as Yee led her by the hand towards the balcony. Every fibre, every muscle, every synapse was begging her to fight, to run, to do anything to avoid what she knew was coming. Then she thought of Jiao, his grin as he'd taken her from her hotel room and carried her to the car by one arm. She knew he would be waiting if she didn't do what Yee wanted. Jiao could make it a lot worse.

Sliding the door open, Yee pushed Isobel gently on to the balcony and followed her out. Isobel shuddered as she imagined Yee's eyes on her body, barely covered by the red dress.

"I've made you a drink," Yee said, handing Isobel a glass. Isobel took it obediently and took a tiny sip, trying not to show the repulsion that surged through her.

"You know, I chose this place for the balcony," Yee said, indicating the view with his glass. "I could have got one higher, but it's too windy up there."

Isobel looked at the row of balconies above, each one precariously jutting from the building. Would anyone up there hear her if she shouted? Would they call the police, or would Yee stop her before it got that far?

"Here I can sit, any time of the day or night, and take in

the city." Yee waved at the view which panned out in front of them.

Isobel stood beside him. She was a few inches taller than Yee even with no shoes on.

A cold finger of wind made her shiver.

Taking a deep breath, Isobel tried to calm herself. Maybe Yee just wanted them to spend some time together?

The thought was shattered as Yee pulled her in front of him.

Isobel felt her pulse rise as his hands explored her body above the dress. She felt him behind her.

Pushing Isobel forwards, across the bar of the railing, Yee's hands moved on to her skin beneath the dress.

Isobel held the railing, trying to concentrate on the city and ignore the unwelcome hands. Every part of her wanted to scream and fight, but there was no one to help her. No one even knew she was here.

Twenty-eight floors below, a family walked from the building, nothing more than distant specks on the concrete. Again, Isobel thought about shouting. Would they hear her?

Isobel wished she was down there, or back in London, anywhere but here.

Yee pulled her dress up. Isobel tried to concentrate on the horizon, ignoring the whipping cold. She hoped it wouldn't last long. It would be over soon, then she'd find a way to escape, to get away, even if it meant prison.

I know I've screwed up, Isobel thought, hearing the sound of Yee undo his belt. *But there must be someone who can help me.*

She held her breath, expecting to feel him at any moment.

There must be someone who can help me.

"There must be someone, help me," she whispered through clenched teeth, only audible by the wind.

211

Her whole body tensed, waiting for him. The colour drained from her knuckles on the railing.

If Yee was going to have his way, he'd have no illusion that she was enjoying it.

Isobel took a deep breath, counting the seconds.

"There must be someone…"

Held breath.

Gritted teeth.

The rumble of the city, so far away.

A doorbell.

Isobel stood motionless, not daring to breathe. Was that the doorbell of Yee's flat? She wasn't sure.

Behind her, Yee grumbled, ignoring the chime.

He continued to rub her body; his hands now felt oily.

The doorbell chimed again.

Yee stopped. Isobel felt him turn.

It chimed again, impatiently.

Isobel heard Yee grumble, pull up and fasten his trousers. Then Isobel heard the door slide open and Yee pad back into the apartment. She took a deep breath. Without turning, she stood up and pulled down the dress. Behind her, the door slid closed and a key ground in the lock.

Chapter 68

Allissa felt the lump in her stomach grow as they reached the 28th floor. Leo rang the doorbell and they heard a sharp but distant chime.

Allissa swallowed; she could still taste the burning dust of the restaurant. She hadn't been able to get the question out of her mind: how had she got it so wrong?

Leo hit the doorbell again. He was getting impatient.

A minute past in painful silence. Allissa watched Leo. Were they too late?

Hearing movement inside, Allissa looked at the door. The bright speck of the viewing hole became dark as someone from the inside looked out at them.

Leo straightened up and forced a smile.

The lock disengaged and the door opened.

Standing in the bright light of the flat, Yee smiled.

"Mr Yee, we need to talk to you," Allissa said, not wasting any time. "It's very important."

Yee didn't reply, and made no attempt to show them into the flat. Allissa stepped forward, but Yee held his ground with the door in one hand and the frame in the other. Yee looked over his shoulder anxiously as though checking something.

"What are you doing here? How do you know my address?"

Yee said. "I thought you had everything you needed from me?"

"This is for your own safety," Leo said, watching Yee closely. "It's about Isobel…"

Yee's eyes darted to the left.

"Earlier today," Leo said, "Isobel tried to kill us."

Allissa looked beyond Yee into the apartment. As though noticing, Yee pushed the door closed so only his outline was visible.

"We've no idea how," Allissa said, "but she's dangerous. We think you may be in danger too."

"I can assure you I'm not," Yee said. "Everything here is fine."

A lift rumbled somewhere, people returning to or leaving their apartments.

"I spoke to Jamie or Isobel or whatever her name is this morning and she's gone," Yee said. "I don't expect to see her again. No one in my company does, so I'd like to get back to…"

"Where is your family?" Leo asked. Yee looked startled by the question.

Yee's expression seemed less sharp than usual; his eyes were hazy and bloodshot.

"They're visiting relatives, but it's none of your business."

"Then you're alone tonight?" Allissa asked.

"Yes, of course, and everything is fine. I don't wish to see you again. Please leave me alone." Yee started to close the door. He already seemed distracted by something in the flat.

Watching the architect push the door shut, Allissa felt her sickening feeling swell. Something here was not right. What was it?

With a pang of regret, Allissa realised her bad decision earlier in the night had clouded her judgement and removed her confidence. Was she just out of her depth?

"We've got this wrong," Leo whispered, as the door began to swing. "Isobel's here."

"What?" Allissa heard the words but they didn't register.

"We've got this wrong," Leo repeated. "You were right, I'm sorry I doubted you."

With that Leo sprung at the closing door, kicking it open a moment before the lock engaged.

In surprise, Allissa followed. A sense of raw emotion welled through her.

"We know she's here," Leo shouted, barging into the flat. He looked around the minimalistic living room.

Yee protested, shouting, attempting to push the pair back out. Leo and Allissa surged forward. Yee slapped with open palms and reddened with exertion.

Leo, ignoring his anxieties that Yee may be some kind of martial arts expert, pushed him to the sofa. The smaller man crumpled, moaning into the leather.

Holding Yee down, Leo looked at Allissa. She stood still, staring at the darkened view of the city through the room's large window.

On the other side of the light-flecked pane, barely visible in the brightness of the room, Isobel pounded the glass.

She looked a mess. Hair wet, face streaked with tears, eyes red and swollen. She was wearing some kind of small dress that barely covered her body.

Seeing the pair notice her, Isobel thumped at the glass with both hands in desperation. The sound was barely audible from inside.

"What has this animal done?" Allissa said, running the two paces towards the window.

Yee muttered to himself and tried to stand. Leo pushed him back down.

As Allissa turned the lock and slid the glass open, the world seemed to come alive. Air from the evening swept in, the rumble and screech of the city and Isobel's shouts of pain and relief.

Allissa knew the world could be cruel and unpredictable. She'd learned that first-hand. She also knew she couldn't fix everything. Somewhere a battle was starting that she or Leo – however hard they worked – would not be able to solve. But taking Isobel in her arms, Allissa felt the overwhelming sense that everything was going work out just fine.

Looking over her shoulder, Allissa knew Leo felt it too.

Noticing Leo's distraction as he watched the two women, Yee climbed to his feet. While Leo was still looking at Allissa who held Isobel, bright against the city below, Yee rounded the sofa. Then he charged at the women, emitting a harsh, horrifying scream.

Allissa was first to react, pushing Isobel out of the way of the running figure. Leo was second, jumping over the sofa behind Yee and shoving him in the direction of the open door.

With flailing arms, Yee flew through the door, colliding with the balcony rail and stumbling to the floor. Allissa stepped forwards before he could turn, slid the glass door, closed it and locked him out.

Chapter 69

"I think this could be the start of something special," Jamie says, looking down at Isobel, unblinking. The wind is cold, but Jamie's hands are warm and wanted. Isobel hasn't kissed anyone for five years. Since what happened at uni.

They share another drink, watching the city from the balcony. They talk. Isobel tells him how she's not been with anyone in a while, after what happened. She doesn't tell him what happened. He doesn't ask.

He lets her talk. Maybe she's drunk; the words are like lubricant. Once they start, she can't stop them. Isobel talks about how long she's worked at the firm, how she's always dreamed of being an architect. How she hopes one day to go back and finish the course.

She doesn't notice his eyes take in her body in the dress. The sound of the city mutes as he pulls her close. Isobel bites her bottom lip.

Jamie says he's seen her around the office. He's liked her for a while. Wanted to get to know her. She smiles in return. No one has spoken to her like this in a long time.

He notices her smile and says how beautiful it is, how it lights up her whole expression. He tells her he really likes how she laughs with her eyes.

"I've wanted to be this close to you for ages," he says. His gaze holds hers. His hand caresses her hip. "You've always given off that vibe… that unapproachable vibe," he says.

Suddenly she's thoughtful.

"It's not a bad thing, it's sexy as hell. I just never thought you were, you know…" His eyes glance at her arm around him.

The silence swells. Kissing makes more sense. Again, it's nice.

"Surely you get chatted up all the time," he says. "When you look this good." He holds her at arm's length.

Isobel shivers as she misses the warmth of his body.

Two women step out on the balcony. One of them rummages for a lighter.

"It's getting cold here," Jamie says, putting his arm around Isobel again. "Shall we go up to my room? I'm staying at the hotel upstairs."

"But, I don't, I'm not…"

"Listen," he says, brushing a strand of hair from her cheek, "I'm not even talking about that. I just feel like I've waited all this time to talk to you. I want this to be the start of something special. I'd just like to spend some time with you, privately."

Isobel thinks about arguing. Jamie leans in and kisses her again.

"Okay." She nods before she realises what she's done.

"I'll just go and pay the tab at the bar and I'll be back. Don't go away. I've been waiting for this for so long."

He puts his hands on her hips.

"I won't," she says. "I won't."

218

Chapter 70

Allissa took Isobel into the bedroom to get changed. They needed to get out of Yee's apartment as soon as possible. The moment Yee was out of sight, Isobel pushed the red dress to the floor.

Through the glass, Yee continued to shout and bang.

Bending to pick up Isobel's clothes, as much as an excuse to look away, Allissa scanned the bedroom. It was austere and plain, like the rest of the apartment.

"This afternoon," Isobel said, taking the clothes from Allissa. "At that restaurant... I... I..."

Allissa looked back at the naked girl clutching the clothes.

"He made me," Isobel said, trying to speak. "I... I..."

"Let's get out of here and then we'll talk. You're safe now," Allissa said, holding Isobel's shoulders. "I promise." Allissa hoped it was a promise she would be able to keep.

Out in the living room, Leo was trying to ignore the frantic little man on the balcony. Yee was now battering the glass with a small table in an attempt to get in.

Just looking at Yee made Leo feel sick. The image of Isobel, destitute, desperate and nearly naked. How could Yee treat someone like that? How could he get enjoyment from that?

Leo knew he couldn't go into the bedroom, Allissa would

219

be getting Isobel dressed. There was an unspoken rule about things like that.

Trying to avoid looking at Yee, Leo's eyes settled on a laptop on the coffee table. It would be locked, surely. Leo picked it up and opened it anyway.

The screen of the laptop sprung to life with the documents Yee had been looking at when he'd last used it. No password. This guy was either very trusting or never let anyone close enough to him to try. Adeptly, Leo scrolled through the open documents on the screen. As he did, the frantic thumping on the glass increased. There was obviously something on the computer that the architect didn't want Leo to see.

Leo minimised two documents containing plans for an apartment building he didn't recognise. There was what looked like a demolition order and a timeline, or schedule, for its redevelopment. One looked like it was a building near the docks. The demolition order was dated for tomorrow and there was a spreadsheet showing the dimensions and cubic capacities of something.

Then, with a pang of sickening recognition, Leo stopped. The next page was titled 'Nathan Mansions Re-development Schedule.' He read on. It was a plan to turn a 'low grade residential property in a prime Kowloon location into 100 high-quality apartments, retail space and a boutique hotel.'

The late-night banging from the thick-necked eviction crew, the crying children, the homeless family. Nathan Mansions was their own home in Hong Kong.

Behind the redevelopment schedule was an e-mail thread with a number of messages and replies. It was, fortunately, in English. It seemed the architect conducted most of his dealings in English.

It was a conversation between Yee and two other people, probably the firm's management team. It seemed to detail the methods they'd used to try to evict the tenants, starting with incentives, and ending in the men Leo and Allissa had seen.

Leo was shocked at how openly Yee and his team discussed these peoples' futures. It was as though they were just an inconvenience to their ambitions.

Leo snuck a look at Yee. For the second time in a few minutes, the small man appalled him.

A noise sounded from the computer on Leo's lap. A new e-mail had been received. Leo clicked on the pop-up and an e-mail thread filled the screen. He began to read, his jaw dropping open as the sickening meaning began to permeate.

Two days ago one member of the conversation had asked what they should do, having tried all the legal and some semi-illegal methods to remove the tenants. Another had replied, "Let's give them the Canton Road Tower treatment?" The question had remained unanswered for almost twenty-four hours until Yee had replied that afternoon with, 'It's arranged. Friday.' The reply, which had just arrived, was a show of approval from one of the members of the e-mail thread.

But what was "The Canton Road Tower treatment?" Leo thought, pulling a browser window open to search.

Chapter 71

It's been a long time since Isobel has felt the warmth of someone's touch on her skin. Standing on the balcony alone, waiting for Jamie to pay the bill, she feels a flutter of excitement. London lies in the background. Taxis scuttle like bugs.

Isobel is looking forward to spending the evening with him. Just to talk, that's what they agreed.

Two minutes later, Jamie's back. Isobel shudders, feeling his hand on her back.

The predator and the prey, ready for the final dance.

They laugh as he leads her towards the lift. They kiss again as they wait.

When the lift arrives, Jamie pushes her against the mirrored back wall and traces her neck with kisses.

Out on the tenth floor they pass a clerk from the hotel. Jamie smiles at him. The accomplice.

Fumbling with a key card, Jamie opens the door. They're in.

"I've had this brought up especially," Jamie says, pointing towards the bottle of champagne on ice and a pair of glasses. "I just feel like this is a celebration, the night we finally got to meet. The start of something amazing."

Isobel glows. They kiss again.

In a few minutes her dress will be on the floor.

Jamie already knows it'll be worth it.

He'll be gone by the time she wakes up.

Chapter 72

In the bedroom Isobel dressed quickly. It felt good to get some comfortable clothes back on. She already felt more able to face the world and couldn't wait to get out of Yee's apartment.

Looking at herself in the mirror above the dressing table, the impact of the last hour was visible. Isobel wore it with patches on her face and the tired, vacant look in her eyes. It felt like she had visibly and physically aged in the time she'd been there. She needed to get out of here.

Just as she was about to turn, Isobel saw something glint in her peripheral vision. A streak of light from the dressing table below. Shiny, gold, inviting. Attracted to it, she looked down. At the back, behind bottles of jars of colourful liquids and creams she saw a ring. An engagement ring – an expensive one. Multiple large diamonds forged onto a dainty gold band.

Picking it up, Isobel saw how it sparkled beneath the light. It was beautiful. Not just one diamond, but many. Watching the colours and hues which sparkled and shimmered in the strong light of the room, Isobel had a thought. Sure, she could take the ring. That would annoy Yee. But the questions his wife would ask if she saw someone else wearing it, that would hurt him even more.

"I'm going to go and see how Leo's getting on," Allissa said, standing from the bed. Isobel had almost forgotten she was there. "Come out when you're ready and we'll get out of here."

"Before you go," Isobel said, speaking as the idea came into her mind. "Could you just help me with something?"

Chapter 73

A moment after pressing enter, Leo saw a hundred horrific images fill the screen.

"Canton Road Tower fire," he said as Allissa sat on the sofa next to him. "This is what Yee plans to do to where we're living." Leo felt a rising fear saying the words.

"'Residents flee burning homes.'" Allissa read one of the articles out loud. "'Number of dead unknown as Canton Road Tower gutted by fire.'"

The article filled the screen. On the top, a large image of a blackened tower block against a blue Hong Kong sky.

"'Canton Road Tower, which caught fire last night, was said to be home to nearly one thousand people...'" Leo read aloud. "'The actual number is unknown as many of the apartments held more than one family due to recent rising rents in the area.'"

He paused to look with disgust at Yee who stared out towards the city.

"Investigators are asking whether the fire alarm system was properly maintained as the fire spread unhindered throughout the building and the fire department was not automatically notified. Investigations are currently on-going."

Leo and Allissa looked at each other as the gravity of Yee's plan sunk in.

"When?" Allissa said.

Leo flicked back to the e-mail thread.

"Friday."

"Tomorrow."

They sat silent for a moment.

The lives and homes of the people they'd seen that morning depended on them. They needed to do something, but what? How could this be stopped?

As Isobel walked in from the bedroom, Leo closed the laptop and got to his feet. They would deal with this, but first they had to make sure Isobel was safe.

Chapter 74

Seeing the ethereal light of the Lucky Cat 24-hour restaurant in Kowloon, Leo realised that he had not eaten in a long time. Allissa and Isobel must be hungry too. If they weren't, the smell of fried beef, oysters and onions which greeted them as they pushed open the door would soon bring it on.

"Three beers please," Leo said to the waitress, raising his voice against the babble of many languages and the hiss of frying food.

"We should leave Hong Kong as soon as possible," Leo said as the waitress left the table. "We don't know what might happen now."

"We'll be alright," Allissa replied. "We'll move to a different hotel. Hong Kong is a big city."

But all Leo could picture was Isobel, helpless and frantic behind the glass an hour ago. There was no telling what Yee's twisted mind was capable of.

"You're going to be alright," Allissa said. Isobel pulled her arms tightly around her and shivered despite the heat of the restaurant.

"If you hadn't…" Isobel stuttered, visibly shaking. "If you hadn't been there… I think he'd have…"

"I know, I know," Allissa soothed, putting a hand on Isobel's shoulder as the waitress brought the beers.

"I've never seen anyone like that before…" Isobel said.

"You're safe now," Allissa reassured her. "We're going to look after you, don't worry."

"But I tried to kill you in the restaurant," Isobel said. "How can you trust me?"

"You were just doing what you were told, you didn't have a choice." Allissa looked closely towards Isobel, her head tilted forward.

"Just promise you won't do that again," Leo smiled.

"I can't believe I did that. What sort of person have I become?" Isobel looked at Leo, her voice softening at his smile. "This isn't me. This isn't the sort of thing I do."

Isobel turned to look through the steamy glass at Kowloon's nocturnal fairground. Leo followed her gaze. Stall holders at the night market across the street talked as they begun to pack their products away.

The roads had quietened but were not empty. People passed flickering neon possibilities of all-night food, drink or sex. *Billions of years of mankind but the basic needs had remained the same.* Leo watched it all from behind his daze of tiredness.

Across the road, he noticed four women straighten up, push out their chests and beam at a group of young men who walked past. The men didn't stop. An older man walking behind them did. He stopped to talk to a girl whose tight green dress exposed an immature figure.

"I just wanted a chance," Isobel said without warning, putting the beer down. "It feels like everything has been against me. Then what happened with Jamie. I was drunk, I know that. But I didn't think… Anyway, I just wanted a chance, and the thought of teaching him a lesson was good too." She spoke as though not used to people listening. Allissa and Leo sat in silence.

"It wasn't meant to go this far," Isobel said. "It was just supposed to teach him that he couldn't be a dick and get away with it. But then it worked, and I thought why not give myself a chance? Let him stay there for a while. I would have owned up. I would have told them it was a mistake, but by then maybe they wouldn't have minded. They would have seen what I was capable of and maybe given me a try anyway."

Leo watched her pause for a drink. He was sure the world didn't work like that. You couldn't just lie to get a job, then say sorry and be kept on. That would never happen.

"I know it sounds crazy," Isobel said, as though reading Leo's thoughts. "But I feel like I've never had that opportunity, things have always been against me. Ever since..." Isobel suppressed a sob. She wasn't going to cry. Not now. "I thought that if I could just try it, just do it, then maybe. I didn't plan for it to go this far."

"What about people at home?" Allissa asked.

"There isn't anyone, really," Isobel replied, her expression dropping. "I don't know my dad and my mum had this new boyfriend who was a total control freak, so we never spoke. When they were first together, I'd go around, but the way he'd look at me just made my skin crawl so I stopped going. Total pervert."

Through the window, Leo noticed the older man finish his negotiation and follow the woman down the street. A bulky man leaning in the shadows moved alongside her and opened a door between two shops. Leo watched through the neon-smeared glass as the door was held open for the older man to follow.

"Then yesterday when Yee found out," Isobel said, staring at, rather than through the window, "he wouldn't let me go. He had that man. They took me to an apartment for the night. I just couldn't get away. I wanted to. He said if I did, he'd report me to the authorities here. That I was committing a very serious crime. I was scared, I didn't know what to do."

Leo watched the bulky man close the door behind the woman and her customer, then step back into the shadows.

"I couldn't get away, I didn't know what to do," Isobel said again, wiping her eyes on her sleeve. "Then he said he had something he wanted me to do. I thought it would be… well… but he said that you were going to be in that restaurant. All I needed to do was lock the door and walk away. He said if I did that, he'd arrange for my flight home."

Isobel paused. Across the table, Leo and Allissa watched her.

"It's okay now," Allissa said again. "You're safe. We know you didn't have a choice."

Isobel looked down at her hands on the table.

"You've just had a really bad run of luck," Allissa said, "and some real dicks have taken advantage of you."

Isobel looked at Allissa, her pale face blotchy in the harsh light of the restaurant. Leo felt for her; it seemed she'd been let down at every turn. Turned away and wronged.

"I want you to go and stay with some friends of mine," Allissa said.

Chapter 75

"Y ou can stay there as long as you want, until you're ready to go back to the UK," Allissa said across the table which was now piled high with bowls of steaming noodles. The intense smell made Allissa realise how long it had been since she'd had a proper meal. They all ate feverishly.

While they had been waiting for the food, Allissa told Isobel the brief story of the guesthouse in Kathmandu. How she owned it, how she'd bought it with money her father had given her, and how it was now run by a charity for women displaced by human traffickers.

"I know that it might take a while," Allissa said between mouthfuls, "but stay as long as you need – you won't be bored there. The girls there are lovely, they'll give you lots to do. Lots to take your mind off things until you're ready to go home."

Isobel looked across the table at her in silence.

"Are you... are you sure?" Isobel said, finally. "But, Kathmandu, that's like in..."

"Nepal," Leo said. "It's only a few hours from here."

"We'll sort your flight out as well." Allissa was aware of the look Leo might be giving her but didn't turn to see it. "We've been paid well to be here," she said, more to Leo than Isobel, "we need to help you."

Isobel didn't say a word, she just nodded towards Allissa and Leo sitting opposite her and forced a smile.

"I'd like to go as soon as possible. I've had it with this place."

Leo pulled out his phone.

"The bus to the airport runs all night from just out there," he said, pointing down the road, "and there's a flight to Kathmandu in five hours."

Dulled by the window, the circus of nocturnal Kowloon didn't stop. Cars continued to stream past, despite the now late hour. Across the street, an old man appeared from a dark doorway between two shops, sauntering towards West Kowloon before disappearing into a side street.

Two minutes later, the girl he'd followed through the door appeared. Fresh-faced and ready. In her endless cycle the night was still young. There was money to be made.

Half an hour later, Isobel, Allissa and Leo stood at the stop for the airport connection bus. High flecks of colour had started to swirl in the clear sky. Dawn was coming and it was going to be a spectacular one.

"Take this," Leo said, passing Isobel a handful of notes he'd just pulled from an ATM on the way. "That'll be enough for your flight."

"I'll get one of the girls to meet you at the airport," Allissa said. "Be prepared though, Kathmandu is a crazy place – but I think you'll like it."

Isobel looked towards them both. She was trying not to cry. She had been holding back the tears for as long as she could remember.

Watching her, Allissa knew what that felt like. The tears

233

must be searing by now.

"Thank you," Isobel said.

"You would do the same if you'd been through what we have," Allissa said. She knew the journey Isobel was on. She knew the memories would have already begun their constant cycle through her mind and that they would continue for a long while yet.

Isobel, with her arms still folded tightly around her, shivered.

"You're cold," Leo said, pulling off the hoodie he was wearing. "Take this, it'll be cold on the plane."

Isobel took the hoodie and smiled as the tears began.

Chapter 76

"You've got two guests staying here, a man and a woman," a voice said across the cramped reception desk of the hotel in Nathan Mansions. The night receptionist looked up from the screen on which a colourful animated video played.

"We have a lot of guests," he said, looking back towards the screen. "Do you want a room?"

"I want to know about these guests," the man said aggressively, sliding a grainy black and white photo across the desk.

The receptionist's eyes widened as a hundred Hong Kong dollar note joined the photo.

"Don't consider my generosity to be a weakness," the man said, sliding another note alongside the first. "If you don't want the money, there are other ways I can get this information from you."

Behind the man, a figure stepped through the door. He was large and wore a dark suit. His powerful hands were balled into fists.

"There are other ways I can get this information," the man at the desk repeated, "but you just telling me and then getting to keep this money is the easiest for us all."

"Room 12," the receptionist said, sliding the notes from the

235

counter, holding them inside his fist and looking again at the computer screen.

"Are they in the room?" the man asked.

"I don't think so, I haven't seen them come past."

"I need a key," the voice said. Two more notes appeared on the counter. It was a lot of money.

The receptionist hesitated for a moment, his eyes on the large, silent figure in the background. Muscles bulging beneath his suit.

"I need a key," the voice repeated.

The receptionist pulled a key card from a box on the desk, programmed it and put it on the counter. Taking the card, the men disappeared into the gloom.

Chapter 77

Isobel had always said she wasn't the sort of person to cry. Some people loved it, get it all out, have a good cry. That wasn't her. She needed to sort things out, to make things better physically.

But standing there, waiting for the bus to the airport, she cried. No one had ever given her their jacket before. No one had cared enough. With that kind gesture from one person to another something inside her broke. Then came the tears.

As they flooded forth, Isobel rolled the hoodie into a ball and pressed it against her face.

She tried to stutter something, but it was inaudible.

Had she ever cried before? She couldn't remember.

She hadn't cried after the terrible night at uni, the one that led her here. She hadn't cried when she had woken up in the hotel room to find Jamie wasn't there after all the sweet and loving things he had said. She hadn't cried when Yee's cold hands explored her body. She didn't cry when Leo and Allissa gave her money for a flight and free accommodation to get her head back in the right place. But now with one tiny gesture of kindness, the tears came.

Allissa was the first in with her arms around her, and Leo followed. They held her for the few minutes until the bus pulled out of the traffic.

"This is you," Leo said, stepping away.

"Yes, I'll…" Isobel stuttered.

"You look after yourself," Allissa said, holding her tight again for a moment.

"Thank you for everything," Isobel said to them both.

Isobel looked towards Leo, now wearing just a T-shirt in the cold morning.

"Take this for the walk home," she said, unzipping and removing the thin sports jacket and putting Leo's on, leaving the hood up.

"Thanks," Leo said, accepting it and draping it around his shoulders.

As the bus accelerated into the swirl of morning traffic, Allissa and Leo watched Isobel's waving silhouette at the window.

Allissa looked at Leo, ridiculous with the tiny girls' sports jacket.

"What?!" Leo said, seeing Allissa's smile.

For the second time that day Allissa stepped close and hugged him. This time Leo was ready.

"You really can change the world with kindness," Allissa said, her voice muffled by his shoulder.

Chapter 78

How could anyone stay in a room like this? he thought, letting himself in. It was tiny, just two single beds against the side with a narrow gap down the middle. It was messy too, clothes were piled up and the beds left unmade.

He squinted into the darkness; only the most persistent light made it through the grime-covered windows and dirty curtains.

The room was empty. Good. He wanted to surprise them. Spring up when they weren't expecting it, see how they liked it.

He had been hoping to find somewhere to hide, revealing his presence when they arrived. The drama of it appealed to him. Looking left and right he saw there wasn't anywhere in the tiny room. Not even a wardrobe.

He removed a small hip flask from his jacket pocket with a gloved hand, unscrewed the cap and took a sip. The strong spirit tasted good. It invigorated him.

To the right, a small door opened into the bathroom. It wasn't really a bathroom, he thought, pushing it open. More like a tiled box containing a toilet and shower.

It would have to do.

In the past, he thought, trying to make himself comfortable, he had gotten someone else to handle things like this. But this one... this one was personal.

It involved the girl.

He'd wanted her for himself and they'd stopped him. He bristled with anger in the darkness. He hated it when people stopped him getting the things he wanted.

Then there was the theft.

Did they think he wouldn't notice? He couldn't let them get away with that.

Feeling anger bristle, he dropped a hand into his pocket and felt the cold metal shape of the gun. He would sort this out, he thought, hearing voices in the corridor outside.

He would sort it out in the way he always did.

Chaos into order. Order where he had control.

Chapter 79

The light of dawn mottled the streets as Leo and Allissa walked back to their hotel.

Leo wanted nothing more than to tell Allissa about the photo. It burned inside him. But it could wait until tomorrow. Right now, tiredness scorched his eyes. All he could think about was sleep.

As they walked, Kowloon started to stir itself awake. Taxis buzzed from street to street, picking up people on their commute to work. The busses, which had been empty an hour before, were now filling up. And the pavements were becoming crowded with people in suits, walking towards the metro stations.

Leo realised it had been nearly twenty-four-hours since he made that walk himself, heading towards The Peak.

The residents of Nathan Mansions were starting to stir, too. People were leaving for work, washing was being hung and floors were being swept.

It was fascinating that this microcosm of life existed within the city. It was so close to the brightly lit towers of glass and chrome, but yet so different. Smiling at two ladies hanging washing, Leo thought of the plans he'd read on Yee's laptop. He still didn't know what they could do to help.

Ahead, a large man walked away, out of sight. His bulky shape strained inside a dark suit. He looked out of place with the residents of the building and something triggered in Leo's memory. Where had he seem him before?

Tiredness, Leo thought, taking the key card from his wallet and unlocking the door to their room. After 24 hours he didn't know what he was seeing.

"I need sleep so much," Allissa said, walking towards her bed in the small room.

Leo put Isobel's sports jacket on a pile of clothes – the room was a mess. They would leave tomorrow.

"I know today has been…" Leo started, but his reply was interrupted by a voice from behind them.

Chapter 80

"You thought you could just leave me there, didn't you?" came the voice. Leo knew who it was before he turned.

"I could have died on that balcony," Yee said, looking towards them both. He seemed to have recovered slightly from his earlier drunkenness. He wore a dark suit, his hair was carefully gelled and in a gloved hand, he held a gun.

Leo had never seen a gun before, other than in films and once when he went clay pigeon shooting.

He'd certainly never had one pointed at him.

Leo was at the back of the room, Allissa slightly in front. Neither spoke.

"You thought you could just walk into my home and ruin my plans," Yee said. "You're not going to get away with that."

Leo and Allissa both stood, facing the man.

Leo spoke first.

"What do you want?"

Maybe it was the madness of no sleep, but Leo felt calm. He knew what he had to do. As he spoke, he took a small step towards Yee.

"First, I want to know where Isobel is," Yee said, seeming not to notice Leo's approach.

"Why do you want to know that?" Allissa snapped.

"It's none of your business why I want to know that," Yee shouted. "I want to know it and you're going to tell me."

Leo thought of Isobel; she'd probably be at the airport now. She wasn't safe yet.

"We don't know. She left," Allissa grunted.

"What do you want with her?" Leo said.

"The three of you have caused me a lot of trouble. A lot of trouble. And now I'm here to tidy up the loose ends, and that includes her," Yee snarled, exposing small, white teeth. "You can't seriously expect to be able to mess up someone's plans and there not be repercussions?"

"Who are you to talk about repercussions?" Allissa said. "Treating a human being like that."

Yee shook his head, ignoring the comment.

"And one of you has stolen from me," Yee said, grimacing.

"What are we supposed to have stolen?" Leo stepped forward again. Allissa did the same. Yee hadn't noticed.

"Someone HAS stolen from me!" Yee was shouting now, the gun shaking.

"What have we stolen?" Allissa repeated, stepping forward again.

"A ring of my wife's. It was in the bedroom on the dresser, but now it's not," Yee said, sounding more pathetic with each statement. Leo and Allissa were getting closer.

"Just go buy another one," Leo said.

"It's been in my family for three generations. It's worth a lot of money – no one knows how much. It can't just be replaced."

"Well, you're not going to find it here," Leo shouted.

At the same time, he and Allissa dove forwards.

Leo lunged for the hand holding the gun and pushed it to

the side. Yee fired. The bullet thudded harmlessly into the concrete wall. Then, knocking Yee off his feet, Leo smashed the gun to the ground. In the commotion Yee let go and the gun skittered beneath one of the beds.

"Jiao!" Yee shouted as Leo held him to the floor.

Allissa grabbed his writhing legs.

"Jiao!" Yee shouted again, followed by words Leo didn't understand.

The door swung open and a long shadow fell across the room.

Looking up, Leo knew what was about to happen. It was a pang of recognition he'd rejected as tiredness. He had seen this man before, in Yee's office.

Leo didn't have time to panic as the dark outline closed in.

The little man on the floor continued to writhe and kick.

As the shadow moved over him, Leo looked up again. A strong arm reached for him.

Leo looked up into Jiao's grinning face as the arm closed around his shoulders. Then he felt the strike on the back of his neck. The world went dark.

Chapter 81

"I don't think I've ever been anywhere as beautiful as this," Leo says, as colour drains from the sky and the noise of the island swells. Birds flash through the twilight, streaks of pink and purple.

"I knew you'd like it," Mya replies in a whisper, kicking water from the ocean. Her feet dangle from the edge of the jetty.

"How did we get here? I mean this is crazy – it's like a different world," Leo says, pointing towards the inky ocean in front of them – undisturbed, unbroken. They've been travelling for two months but this is the first time they've seen an ocean like this. An expanse of boundless blue.

A bird squawks, the light of a boat creeps across the horizon.

"Kao Tao is special because it's hard to get to. When things are hard to find – that's when they're precious," Mya says, her voice private and sexy.

She looks out into nothing, her hands on the side of the jetty and her feet swinging freely. She looks beautiful in the way confident people do. Her smile is currency all over the world.

"I'm just glad to be here… with you," Leo says, looking at her profile in the glow of the dim light. "Even the extra month.

I'm so happy to be here."

This is the time, he knows it, tonight. He's had the ring hidden in his wallet for over a month now, waiting for tonight. This time, this place, this girl.

Mya turns to face Leo as he lies backwards on the jetty. Water slaps the supports under the platform. Somewhere nearby, people speak in an unknown language.

"I've never been anywhere as beautiful as this," Leo says, resting up on his elbows. *Now would be the perfect moment.*

Mya leans forward.

"To be… to be here with you is so special…" Leo says.

Mya looks down towards him – her eyes dark, glinting, mysterious, mocking.

"…and we, I mean I, hadn't even planned to come here…"

"Yeah, it's been great," Mya says, turning back to the water. A chill passes across her body, blowing her loose-fitting top tight against her profile. Leo's eyes follow, he can't help it.

He turns and fumbles the ring from his wallet while Mya looks out at the ocean. *This needs to be perfect*, he thinks, *it will be perfect.*

He breathes in deeply. Inhales the sea air, the smell of tamarind, lime, of love, hope and opportunity. Then lets it go.

"Will you marry me?" Leo says, looking towards her. The one-kneed stance tradition dictates not possible on the jetty. The setting and moment will make up for it, he hopes.

An eddy of wind skips past, rushing towards the curving palm trees on the shoreline. The bay shivers. Time hangs. Leo holds his breath, unblinking.

"I…" Mya says, following a train of thought, but cutting it before it starts. She looks from Leo's expectant expression to the ring in his hands.

"Oh my gosh, that's so beautiful." She plucks it from his fingers and holds it up. The colours of twilight refract through the diamonds. To Leo, it seems like an age has passed.

"Come back to the cabin in five minutes," Mya says, climbing to her feet. "Then you'll get your answer."

Leo watches the sparkle of her eyes as she stands, turns away and starts to walk towards the land.

Settling back on his elbows and watching the bruised horizon, Leo shakes his head. He tries to ignore the pangs of disappointment.

That's so typical of Mya, he thinks, watching the silhouette of her shape cross the causeway to the beach. *Doing things her way.*

Chapter 82

Allissa was the first to come around. She wasn't sure how long she'd been out or exactly what had happened.

She'd seen Jiao barge into the hotel room, knock Leo unconscious with ease, and then close in on her. She'd tried to fight, giving up Yee's ankles as she did, but it was no good. Jiao weathered the two or three punches she got in without a reaction and closed in on her in the corner of the room. Her arm went limp as he put pressure on her shoulder and then she followed Leo into the blackness.

There was movement and talking, she was sure of it. Who it was and where they were going, she had no idea.

Allissa opened her eyes slowly. They were not in their hotel room. Looking around she took in the large, bare concrete space, perhaps the entire level of a building. Pillars jutted from floor to ceiling and light flooded from a wall of windows on one side.

Leo lay next to her on the hard, dusty floor. His chest rose and fell and a dark bruise began to form on his neck.

At first, Allissa thought it could be a new building, one of Yee's projects. He must have access to many. But why would he have brought them here? Something didn't fit. She'd seen buildings go up, there were always walls, wires and pipes being installed. They weren't left empty like this.

Allissa made it to her feet and walked, shakily at first, across to the window. The glass was covered by a thick layer of dust and grime. It was not new.

Through the murky glass, the view was unlike any Allissa had seen of Hong Kong. The industrial landscape of the city's docks. Monolithic ships rested in shimmering inlets of water. Above them cranes sat like vultures, some eerily still, others working to remove or add containers in a pattern of balance and weight.

Looking down, Allissa saw the water, sluggish and grey. The building was right against the water. No doubt to give the business that once occupied it a first-hand view of the activity outside. From the drop she estimated they were on the third or fourth floor. There was no way she could tell whether that was the top floor, or if there were twenty more above.

"Where are we?" said a groggy voice from behind her. Leo was coming around too. "Shit, my head."

Allissa turned and saw him sitting up, rubbing his head and neck.

"Somewhere near the docks. I'm not sure where, or why."

"This guy's hospitality is second to none," Leo said, looking around. "Where's the buffet?"

Leaving the window, Allissa walked across to a pair of double doors at the other side of the space. They too looked old, the circular windows thick with dust. She pulled the handle, the door moved slightly and then jarred with the crunching sound of a chain. Pulling again, she looked through the thin column which opened between the doors. There was a chain on the other side, locking the doors together.

"We're locked in," she shouted across to Leo, her voice echoing.

"What is this place?"

"I'm not sure, but I'm not feeling it. We need to find a way out. You take that side of the room, look for anything that might help us."

Rubbing the back of his head, Leo walked across the space.

"There's only one door," he shouted back. "One way in, one way out."

Allissa looked around. The place had a disconcerting quiet about it.

"It must have been some kind of office," she said. "Probably owned by one of the shipping companies, but why has Yee brought us here?"

They didn't have to wait long for the question to be answered. The voice came from behind them, but it wasn't Yee – it was much worse.

"The scheduled demolition of this building will begin in twenty minutes. Please leave now."

Chapter 83

A soap-soaked sponge ran down the window, streaking the world with a white line before being wiped clear. The two men cleaning the window chatted as they switched from sponge to brush and back again. The windows to the left were speckled with dust, to the right they gleamed with the new day.

Isobel looked at the window rather than through it. Cleaning the windows on Hong Kong's International Airport would be a lifetime's work. A job that was never finished. They kept the view of the city sharp for people seeing it for the first time.

No matter how much the window was cleaned, Isobel felt as though she viewed the world through a darkened lens. The last twenty-four-hours just added another painful twist to her life.

How had this happened to her? How had her life gone like this? She knew she was capable, clever and hardworking, but there always seemed to be something that went wrong, or someone who was there to mess it up.

She could pinpoint the night it began. The night her life was changed forever.

Isobel had always wanted to be an architect. To design and create things that would last for generations, combine function with imagination and possibility. The thought had always excited and intoxicated her.

At school people had laughed at her.

"That's a boy's job," the girls teased with their popular dreams.

Isobel had been an awkward teenager. Pale, freckled skin, ginger hair, braces. She'd been teased for it. Teasing that quickly became part of her life. She just got used to it. It was part of who she was.

Once, someone said that no one would every fancy her. After that she decided she didn't want anyone to fancy her. She was good enough on her own. What would she want with another person?

Then, while at university something changed. Men started looking at her differently. She seemed to grow into her body – and everyone noticed, apart from her.

She was used to being the girl who was friends with guys, nothing more. That was the way she liked it.

Isobel had gone to university to get the job she wanted, to follow the dream she wanted. Nothing else.

She got through the first year in the way she always had, registering the looks from her male course-mates without trusting or engaging in them. She went out occasionally but spent the time exclusively with friends. This only seemed to increase their interest.

Did she have a boyfriend at home? Did she think she was just better than them?

She was there to get the qualifications. This was her life and she wanted to make her dream come true.

But people couldn't see that.

A month before her final exams they went out for one of her

housemate's birthdays. Isobel didn't want to go. She wanted to get an early night as she needed to do well.

"But everyone's going. You need to be there."

Finally, she agreed, she'd come for a bit.

They were drinking in a bar when they'd met a group of lads the birthday girl knew. There must have been twenty of them altogether.

Loud music. The drinks kept coming. As soon as one was gone, another came.

By midnight Isobel had to leave.

Stumbling out into the night, she tried to walk bleary-eyed up the hill towards home.

"Let me walk you back," one of the lads said. A guy from her course, she knew him. He was alright. She wasn't in the state to argue.

Back at the house he came in. She hadn't invited him but hadn't said no either.

What happened next was painfully clear.

Chapter 84

"Demolition will begin in twenty minutes. Please leave now."

When the echoes faded to silence Leo and Allissa looked at each other in panic. It was coming from a small speaker attached to the wall above the door. It repeated the message three more times in other languages, echoing fitfully around the room.

"How do they demolish buildings like this?" Leo asked, already knowing the answer.

A moment's silence.

"Explosives," Allissa said, her expression becoming grey.

"I saw a demolition order for a building near the docks on Yee's laptop yesterday. I didn't read it closely, but I bet this is it."

For thirty seconds the pair stood, looking from each other to the small speaker.

Leo had seen it on TV. An old building, an excited commentator, surrounding streets emptied. A countdown. Explosions rippling across the structure. The thing that was so tangible and strong collapsing in on itself in a cloud of dust.

"Where are the explosives?" Allissa asked, moving back over to the window.

"I'd say most of them are in the basement, with a few on the upper floors to make sure the middle collapses first," Leo answered. He didn't know where the answer came from or if he was right but it sounded logical.

"We're going to get out of this," he said, forcing a smile and turning to look at Allissa. "We've come through worse. We will show that shit what's what."

"Of course," Allissa said. "The way I see it, there are two ways out of this room, and the easiest is going to be the door. It's only the handles that are attached together, it can't be that secure."

At the door they held onto a handle each. The grimy metal was cold.

"On my count, pull as hard as you can," Allissa said, before counting down from three.

The door opened an inch until the chain bit. It wouldn't move any further.

"Try again," Leo said. "We might be weakening it."

Again, they did, with no success.

"The scheduled demolition of this building will begin in fifteen minutes," the voice again chimed. They'd been pulling at the door for five minutes and had gotten nowhere.

"This isn't working," Allissa said, "plus there might be other locked doors beyond this one."

"You're right. Let's have a look at the windows," Leo said, leading the way to the wall of glass behind which the world seemed unchanged.

The glass was thick, Leo noticed running a finger across it. He barged it with his shoulder – it seemed to bend.

"I reckon we could break this," Leo said, looking down at the oily water lapping forty feet below. He felt anxiety build in his throat. The water was their only chance, he would have to do it.

But…

But…

With a hand on the glass to steady himself, he counted his breathing.

Five seconds in. Five seconds out.

Breathe in, and out.

"I'll look for some kind of damage, where the glass is weakened," Allissa said, pulling Leo's focus from the water below. Allissa looked concerned. They didn't have time. Leo knew he needed to focus.

Breathe in, and out.

Leo caught another glimpse of the water. He'd have to jump in there.

Five seconds in. Five seconds out.

"You go and look for something to break the glass with," Allissa said, putting her hand on Leo's shoulder and turning him away from the window.

Breathe in, and out.

"Yes, good idea," Leo said. The anxiety subsided slightly when he wasn't looking at the menacing ripple of the water below.

Walking into the room, Leo looked around. Almost everything had been cleared from the building. On the far wall, he noticed a steel angle bracket sticking out from the concrete. It had been used to fit something to the wall. Leo pulled it, it wobbled and the concrete surrounding the fixing bolts started to crack.

He pulled again and it loosened further. It was a heavy bit of metal. Discoloured after years of use but strong. Leo pulled again, putting his whole weight onto the bracket. With a crack, it separated from the concrete but still refused to give completely. He was about to try again when the voice returned.

"The scheduled demolition of this building will begin in ten minutes."

Leo looked over at Allissa who was searching the glass for cracks or dents where it had already been damaged. They could make all the difference.

Keeping her image in his mind, Leo turned back to the bracket. He put both hands up, gripped the rough surface and pulled.

With a jerk downwards, Leo felt the bracket move. He pulled again, and the thing started to move.

He pulled until he felt the steel cut into his fingers. He pulled it until his teeth were clenched and his stomach ached. With a final effort he felt it separate and thud to the floor, along with a lump of concrete loosened over years of use. The extra weight would help.

"Found anything?" Leo asked, carrying the steel bracket over to the window.

"There's a couple, yeah. This one is the most damaged."

Allissa pointed out a pane in the middle which bore a collection of deep-looking cracks.

"That'll do," Leo said. "We don't have time to keep looking."

Trying to ignore the water lapping below, Leo raised the steel bracket above his head. Aiming for the damaged section of glass, he let it fall. The vibrations of the crack stung his elbows. The web of cracks spread across the glass. Dust flew.

Again, he lifted the steel bar and smashed it into the glass. The cracks spread further.

Again. There were lines now reaching to the corners of the pane, but still no hole.

Allissa took the bracket from Leo and turned it around. Using the pointed end, she pushed the centre out. The glass in the middle fell away, leaving a hole where the wind whistled through. She pushed out as much as she could before the glass became solid again. Then turned the bracket around and struck the glass twice more.

"The scheduled demolition of this building will begin in five minutes," the voice behind them said. Neither paid it much attention now – every second counted. The hole was still only two feet across.

"Keep going," Allissa said, passing the bracket back to Leo. After a couple of strikes the steel and concrete felt heavy.

"We need to open it up more to get through."

Allissa concentrated on the edges, knocking shards of glass out which fell towards the murky water below. The hole was widening, but time was ticking.

They looked at each other as the emotionless voice spoke again.

"The scheduled demolition of this building will begin in two minutes."

Chapter 85

The broken glass on the kitchen floor told a different story. So did the bruises on her thighs and arms. So did the smashed lock on the bathroom door where Isobel had tried to seek refuge.

Twenty people had seen them leave the bar arm in arm. Apparently, she had been leading the way. Leading him back to her house where she had opened the door and let him in.

No charges could be brought. The university refused to expel him.

Isobel had tried to go back to complete the course, but she couldn't. She couldn't be there with him and his friends. She had to go, she had to leave.

Initially her family had been good to her. She went back to stay with her mum and step-dad for a while.

Soon, it became clear she was getting in the way.

"Why don't you go back and finish the course? Only a couple of years to go. You've paid all that money."

But Isobel knew she couldn't. There was no way she could sit in the same room as him. Even thinking they could meet as she walked around the city was too much.

Again, she left and within a month had a job at a firm of architects in London. It wasn't as an architect, but it was a good start.

"Passengers for the Cathay Pacific flight to Kathmandu please make your way to the gate. Boarding is about to start." An announcement rang through the airport.

Outside, the light had turned from plum to orange, the day was now out in full glory. The sky was streaked with stratus, as though it was in the process of being cleaned too. Isobel looked out the window at the lines of aircraft. Each multi-coloured tail was an opportunity and soon she would be on one of them. Leaving for Kathmandu.

Chapter 86

"The scheduled demolition of this building will begin in two minutes."

The system was designed so that anyone left in the building got out in time. Providing they could. From behind the cordon marking the safe distance, Yee smiled to himself. The cycle was moving. Something old was being destroyed and making room for something new. Resurrection and decay. This one was particularly special though because two other problems were being solved at the same time.

Yee had never let people take advantage of him or stand in the way of what he wanted. That would have been made clear last night if Leo and Allissa hadn't interfered. But that didn't matter now that Isobel was gone. The ring was gone too. That didn't really matter either. The important thing was the two people who could incriminate him wouldn't be seen again.

What was left of their bodies may be found when demolition crews sorted through the wreckage, but there was no way they could be traced back to him.

"They must have been sleeping there, people with nowhere to stay," he'd say. "We did everything we could, all regulations were followed. It's a terrible accident."

"The scheduled demolition of this building will begin in

one minute and thirty seconds," the voice chimed again.

Jiao stood next to him, scanning the landscape. The building was isolated against the docks behind it. If, through some miracle, Leo and Allissa managed to escape, the only way they could walk to safety was by coming this way. Yee knew that Jiao would be more than ready to finish the job if needed. He had wanted to earlier. Yee had said no. That wasn't the right way to do it.

"What if they manage to break through the wall?" Jiao had asked. That had made Yee laugh. "What do these idiots know about breaking through walls?" he'd replied, kicking Leo in the ribs.

Perhaps two years ago he would have been right. Perhaps two years ago Leo didn't know anything about breaking through walls. But since then he had broken through the expectations of his family. Broken the reach of an overbearing and bullying employer. Broken through the traps set by Lord Stockwell to find and escape with Allissa.

Allissa, on the other hand, through no choice of her own, had spent her whole life breaking through walls. Both the walls set by society on her as a woman. In her family by having a different mother. In herself with her long inability to trust and settle.

In truth, the two young people, currently battering their way out with a steel bar, knew more about breaking through walls than anyone could imagine. For them, it had become a way of life.

Chapter 87

"The scheduled demolition of this building will begin in one minute," echoed the emotionless voice.

The glass was now so damaged that it was falling loose with ease. Leo and Allissa pushed sections of it out frantically as the time counted down. The hole was still not quite big enough. Allissa had the steel bracket while Leo punched and kicked it, ignoring the pain which rose from his fists. They needed the gap wide enough so that they could jump cleanly through it. A caught foot or hand would be enough to ruin the fall and fling them back against the building on the way down.

"The scheduled demolition of this building will begin in thirty seconds," the voice said, in the same electronic nonchalance as it had for the last twenty minutes. They kept pushing. The hole was now about four feet across.

"That'll do, I think," Allissa said, expecting the voice to echo away. It didn't. Now the countdown had started.

29

"I need to tell you something," Leo said, looking towards Allissa.

28

"What, right now?" Allissa pushed the last pieces of glass

out.

27

"I can't swim," Leo said.

26

Allissa looked at him. If she thought it was unusual, she didn't let it show.

25

"Don't worry about it. When you hit the water let yourself float to the top and then kick your legs to stay there."

24

23

"But what..." Leo stuttered. The drop was nothing. It was the oily unwelcoming water that made his breathing quicken.

22

"I'll go first," Allissa said, "and then as soon as you land, I'll come and get you. We will be fine."

21

Leo nodded. He knew there was only one way out of the building. Leo held Allissa's arm as she climbed through the gap and stood on the tiny ledge which protruded at the bottom of the glass pane. To slip now would mean falling down the surface of the building and hitting the concrete lip of the dockside which jutted out just above the water.

20

Forty feet of air and water one way. Steel, glass and concrete the other.

"Just get back up to the surface," Allissa said. "Keep kicking and don't panic. You'll be okay."

19

Crouching on the ledge, Allissa paused for a moment and looked out to the horizon.

18

Then without hesitation, she jumped.

17

16

Time moved quickly. Leo couldn't watch her fall, he hoped she'd landed and was able to swim well enough.

15

14

13

Laying the steel bracket they'd used to make the hole across the inside of the window, Leo stepped out onto the ledge.

12

11

10

On the outside of the building the wind whipped furiously.

9

8

The voice seemed like a whisper now.

7

6

Crouching as Allissa had done, Leo readied himself to jump.

5

He planned to curl into a tight ball, diving was too risky. Landing on your belly at this height could break bones.

4

No time to think about it. No time to worry whether Allissa had made it. To consider whether she'd be there to pull him to the surface. He had to go.

3

2

Jump.

Chapter 88

The Cathay Pacific flight to Kathmandu banked hard above Hong Kong. Below, the city spread out, clinging to the land as though fighting for space between the glinting water. The occasional cloud skipped past as the plane gained altitude.

It felt good to be leaving. A new city, a new chance. Isobel was determined to make this one work. She had the opportunity that Leo and Allissa had given her. The money to get to Kathmandu and the promise of accommodation at the guesthouse. She wasn't sure how long she would stay. She would see how long she needed. At least a couple of weeks.

She also had her backup. The ring. Of course, while in Yee's bedroom Isobel had been scared and shaken. But not shaken enough to ignore the ring on the dresser. It looked expensive and, knowing Yee, it would be.

The moment ran through Isobel's mind again. She'd picked up the ring again after Allissa left the room. Its multiple diamonds glinted an ethereal blue in the bright overhead lights. Then, with thoughts of revenge fluttering through her chest, she'd slid it into the pocket of the black sports top.

Then realisation dropped on her like a stone.

The sports top she'd swapped with Leo.

Chapter 89

L eo didn't remember hitting the water. He remembered the rush of the fall. The tension in his muscles as he pulled his arms and legs in tight.

Then the world went dark and silent.

A moment later he was gasping for breath. Trying to open his eyes in dark water. He was alive, conscious, which way was up? Where did he need to go?

He felt the panic rise as he tried to reach out to grab something. Something to pull him out of the water.

Kicking his legs frantically, he tried to make it back to the surface.

Then he remembered Allissa's final words before she jumped.

"I'll come and get you, don't panic."

Letting himself float for a moment he kicked up towards the hazy, sparkling light of the surface.

Then he was out. Gasping big breaths of beautiful air. Salt, diesel, dust. He could smell and taste them all. He was alive.

He was disorientated too. Water lapped around his ears as he strained to keep his nose and mouth above the waves.

Twice, a wave broke over his face and he swallowed a mouthful of rank, salty water.

Where was Allissa? How long could he keep this up? He couldn't seem to kick hard enough to even see the side of the dock, let alone if Allissa was nearby.

His arms flailed uselessly by his sides as the weight of his wet clothes dragged him down.

What about the building? It still loomed above him. Surely the explosion was meant to have happened by now.

"Don't panic," Leo said to himself, trying to drown out the noise of the thumping water and the screaming anxiety.

"Don't panic."

Leo thought about how easy it was to say that when you're safe.

"Don't panic."

But when you're being dragged beneath the water in the shadow of a building which is due to explode at any second, it's much harder.

Another wave broke over his face, soaking his eyes and filling his lungs.

"Don't panic!" his mind was shouting now.

Then something was dragging him. Not dragging him down, but away from the building. He felt the solidity of an arm around his chest and the movement of someone behind him.

As Allissa pulled Leo through the dark water, she looked up at the building above them. It was at least ten stories, each of them empty. Each of them ready to be dust. Explosions started to flicker across the concrete. Allissa kicked harder, dragging Leo through the water as the flashes started on the ground floor and moved out to the edges. The outline of the building held for a moment, as though fighting the inevitable, floating on air.

Leo was kicking now too, helping them move away.

A rumble seemed to echo from the water. A distant thud and crack. Then the middle of the building started to fall. Floors buckled and twisted, columns bent and distorted and dust swelled from all sides.

Chapter 90

Yee felt an incomparable happiness as he saw the building sparkle and then tumble into rubble. He had always felt the destruction of a building – the flash of light, crack of explosives, the moment of stillness and then the inevitable drop in a billow of dust – as dramatic and glamorous. He'd seen it many times over his career and it never failed to impress him.

As the dust began to settle, Yee removed the hard hat, ran his fingers through the gel of his hair, and turned towards the waiting car.

Jiao got in the other side.

"I'd love to stay and help clean up," Yee said with a smirk, as he watched a group of men walk towards a dormant line of diggers and bulldozers. "But we've got other fires to fight. Have you got everything you need?"

"Yes, everything's in the back," Jiao said, rubbing his thick hands over the trousers of his suit.

"Excellent, let's go. Nathan Road Mansions," Yee said to the driver who slid the car into gear and started in the direction of Kowloon.

Chapter 91

"Bloody lucky we got out," Allissa said, pulling them up to a dirty metal ladder on the dockside.

Leo reached out and pulled himself up on the lowest rung.

"Totally." Leo felt shaky with adrenaline as he watched the cloud of dust begin to settle across the water.

They had been too close. Close enough for the explosion to leave their ears ringing and to taste concrete dust in their mouths. Close enough for it to have ended up very badly indeed.

Watching the swirling dust, Leo remembered the pictures of a completely different kind of demolition on Yee's laptop. A tower gutted by fire, charred from the street to the sky. But this tower was not an empty building. It was not one that had been stripped and left for dead. It was a home to the families they'd been staying beside. Over the last few days, Leo and Allissa had woken to the sound of their children playing, watched them sit down for dinner and smiled good mornings as they'd passed.

Pulling himself up the oil-soaked ladder, Leo knew they didn't have much time. Yee was planning the fire today, but when specifically, he didn't know.

"I don't think he'd do them both at the same time," Leo said as they ran towards a road. Traffic teamed past on the other side of a rusted wire fence.

"Yeah, he'd want to be there. He'd want to watch."

Reaching the fence, Leo pulled up the loose, broken wire. Allissa crawled under and then held it up for him.

Allissa held up her hand towards the speeding traffic. Almost at once a yellow taxi pulled up.

"Nathan Mansions, Nathan Road," Allissa said getting in first. The driver unhappily noted their wet clothes as the water from the dock started to soak into the seats.

"Quickly," Allissa said, pointing towards the road ahead. "It's urgent."

Chapter 92

Arriving outside Nathan Mansions, Yee instructed his driver to pull up onto the kerb on the opposite side of the road. He wanted to watch this. He wanted a front row seat as the residents scurried for their lives carrying whatever pathetic possessions they could manage.

He knew that after the destruction, after the building was useless and no one cared about it, the city would beg him to regenerate it. They would beg him to turn it into one of the buildings they were so proud of.

Getting out the car and pulling a large bag from the back, Jiao crossed the road.

Watching him go, Yee sat back. It was impressive, he thought, how much destruction could fit into one small case. If you knew what to do with it.

* * *

"What they're going to do," Leo said, "is disable the alarms and then start the fire in one of the flats."

"Yeah, but that wouldn't make it catch to all the others. How are they going to make it widespread?" Allissa thought out loud in the back of the taxi speeding towards Nathan Road.

274

The driver's irritation at the wet seats had evaporated at the soggy hundred-dollar-bill now drying on the passenger seat.

"Gas," Allissa said, thinking about the explosion in the restaurant.

"Yes. He'll disable the alarm, fill the place with gas, and then..."

The taxi swung onto Nathan Road. They were three blocks away.

"We'll need to be quick," Allissa said. "I bet the alarm system will be on the ground floor, as well as a gas isolation valve. We need to get our passports and stuff from the room too. If Yee finds out we're out of that building, he'll finish the job properly."

"You run up to the room," Leo said. "Tell everyone you meet there's a fire. Try and spread a bit of early panic and get people out fast. Grab the things we need. I'll search the ground floor for the alarm control and the gas main switch."

"Fine," Allissa replied. "This is it, driver." They were approaching the front of the building. "Just here."

"If you see anyone with a phone who speaks English, get them to call the fire service," Leo said.

Allissa looked at him, as if he'd gotten something wrong.

"What, how can we explain if they don't?"

"Driver," Allissa said. "There's a fire in this building, I need to use your phone." As the taxi driver turned, Allissa pointed at his phone attached to the dashboard.

The driver thought for a moment, looked at the hundred-dollar-bill on the passenger, then passed the phone to Allissa.

Her eyes met Leo's for a second before she dialled the international emergency number and reported a fire at Nathan Road Mansions, Nathan Road, Hong Kong.

Chapter 93

It really is disgusting, Yee thought, looking at the building that was about to be taken over by flames. How could something this horrible be designed? How could it be allowed in this city? His city?

Yee felt repulsed by the cracked, grimy windows, the random assortment of discoloured air-conditioners and the green stains across the concrete. How could people live like this?

As his eyes dropped across the building, he saw people coming and going from the main entrance.

This could be so much more, he thought to himself, a prickle of irritation rising as he watched the flow of people. *When these people are no longer in the way, it will be so much more.*

Then he saw something which made him sit upright in the car seat. It couldn't be. How could it be? Was he seeing things? How could Allissa and Leo be here when they were supposed to be under a thousand tons of concrete?

Chapter 94

Jiao had to work quickly. His first task was to disable the alarm system. The controls were hidden behind a panel next to the elevators. If you didn't know what to look for, you would miss it entirely. Two people queuing for the lifts watched as Jiao tried to pull the door open. It was locked. Strange. It had been open last time Jiao had visited to check things over.

Reaching down to his bag on the floor, he pulled a screwdriver from one of the side pockets. Jamming it between the door and the wall, he started to pry it open. The metal started to bend.

"Hey, what are you doing?" a voice speaking Cantonese came from behind him. "Are you authorized to be touching that?"

Jiao turned to see one of the building's security guards looking at him. The man was obviously taking a break from telling people not to drop litter. His blue shirt was pressed neatly and he carried a cap beneath his arm.

Jiao didn't answer, just waited for the smaller man to approach. As he did, Jiao could see the perspiration on his forehead.

"Well? Can I see your authorization?" the smaller man said.

Jiao said nothing, a grin parting his lips.

Reaching out as though to shake the man's hand, Jiao grabbed him by the wrist. Tightening his grip, Jiao watched the man's eyes draw wide with pain and his face redden. Squeezing to the point just before he'd expect to hear bones crack, Jiao nodded at the man. The man nodded back frantically, pleadingly.

Letting the hand go, it fell limp to the man's side. Jiao watched the smaller man's eyes become watery before he turned and scurried away.

He may be back with others, but Jiao would be gone by then. Picking up the screwdriver, Jiao changed tactic. He didn't have much time. Instead of just trying to pop the lock, he worked on bending the metal hinges out of place. In seconds, the twisted metal panel fell to the floor, exposing the fire alarm system.

The system was old and probably didn't work anyway. Various modules were connected with wires and the whole thing was covered with a layer of filth. Jiao knew what to do. First, he ran a finger across the isolation switches, cancelling any signals which may be received by the sensors. Then he pulled out the cable connecting it to the telephone network. Even if it sounded, the fire service wouldn't be called. The fire alarm system would be good for nothing now.

Then Jiao turned towards the stairs. The first flat he needed to visit was on the second floor.

* * *

In the car, Yee fumed. It was them. Definitely. But how could they have survived? They were supposed to be in the building.

He had put the chain on the doors himself. There was no other way out. What were they doing here?

The back of his neck prickled with perspiration.

This wasn't supposed to happen. This could ruin everything.

With a growl, Yee pulled out his phone. They would have to get things started now. It might make it more difficult, but they couldn't wait. That pair could ruin everything. Yee hated it when other people got involved in his stuff.

Yee dialled Jiao. The plan could not be allowed to fail.

Holding the phone to his ear, Yee felt the seat next to him vibrate. Next to him, Jiao's phone slid across the leather.

The idiot. How could he have…?

With another growl of frustration, Yee realized there was only one thing for it. Nothing could get in the way of the plan, not this time.

"Stay here," Yee shouted at the driver before opening the door and stepping into the muggy afternoon.

* * *

On the second floor, Jiao unlocked the padlock and removed the chain which sealed the door. The apartment had been empty for two months. The air was stale and dust lay thick across the counter in the small kitchen. Jiao remembered evicting the people from the apartment. They were an old couple who had begged to stay. They said it had been their home for thirty years. Pathetic.

Jiao got to work straight away. He slid the small cooker away from the wall and pulled the gas hose from its connection. It started to hiss. It was a smaller feed than in the restaurant but would only take a few minutes to fill the small space. Twenty minutes, Jiao thought, removing one of the detonation devices from the bag and setting the timer. They'd worked so well during the trial in the restaurant yesterday, he couldn't wait to see them in action today.

Chapter 95

Nothing was different on the ground floor as Leo and Allissa ran up the steps. Stall holders shouted at meandering people for sales and residents milled about. The effect was boisterous, noisy but reassuring.

Allissa ran for the stairs. She couldn't wait for the elevator. She needed to get their stuff, passports, money, and get out.

Leo's first job was to find the control panel for the alarm system. If he could sound the alarm, people would at least have some warning. It wouldn't save their homes, but it might save some lives.

Feeling his pulse thump in his ears, pleading with his growing anxiety to stay under control, Leo checked the entrance area. He couldn't see a suitable place for the control system. The area was covered with adverts for the stalls within the mall and the names of the hotels above. It was unlikely they would have been put on top of the alarm system.

Running into the mall, Leo scanned every bare section of wall. The control would need to be easy to access. First, he walked around the outer edge of the building. In one corner a security guard sat behind a small desk, cradling his arm. Leo thought for a moment about telling him but doubted he would understand.

When he'd done a whole circuit of the outer wall with no luck, Leo headed for the elevators and stairs in the centre.

Rounding the corner, almost knocking into a pair of tourists walking towards the street, Leo looked around. The area was busy with people coming and going from the elevator doors which slid open and closed constantly. Most of the space on the surrounding walls was empty.

Then he noticed it. On the wall, beside one of the dirty sliding doors, a panel had been left open. The twisted metal of the door seemed to be on the floor below.

That must be it.

Leo peered at the electrical system inside. There was a mesh of wires and modules from which numerous lights and buttons flashed. Leo looked closely from one control to the next. With the Chinese characters, knowing what the buttons did was impossible. Some were in the on position, others in the off, but their function to Leo was a mystery.

At the bottom of the console there was a large red button.

What's the worst that could happen? Leo thought, biting his lip in concentration.

Chapter 96

Yee heard the alarm sound as he ran around the balcony of the fifth floor. He hadn't seen Jiao yet, which was good. He must be on the higher floors.

Jiao was going to set detonation devices in ten apartments, most of them on the lower floors. All of them homes from which they had evicted people.

Heading for the stairs, Yee saw a pair of women sauntering around the balcony. The ringing alarm was having no effect on their speed.

This is why people get killed, he thought, *because they don't pay attention*. Sure, he wanted to destroy their homes, but he didn't want to kill them. If they didn't get out soon, that's what would happen.

Supressing a strange feeling of guilt, Yee headed for the next staircase. Nothing was going to stop this plan.

* * *

On the eighth floor, Allissa heard the shriek of the alarm. Its two-tone undulating whine seemed to get beneath the skin of anyone in its radius. It certainly worked for her as she stuffed their clothes into the bags as quickly as possible. She'd already made sure she got their phones, travel documents and money. It was lucky Yee had left it all there, but then why would he move anything when he didn't think they'd be returning?

Pushing the last few items in, doing up the backpacks and sliding one over each shoulder, Allissa half-walked, half-stumbled to the door. There, she turned to scan the small room. On the floor, by one of the bed side tables lay something dark and crumpled. She didn't recognise it at first.

Cursing under her breath, Allissa put the bags down. It might be important. Stepping back across the room, she picked it up. It was the sports jacket Isobel had given Leo at the bus stop.

While turning it in her hands, Allissa heard something fall to the floor. Something had dropped from the jacket.

The sound was nothing more than a drop of rain against a window, but it got Allissa's attention.

Scanning the floor Allissa saw, glinting in the dull yellow light of the room, a ring.

Chapter 97

With the sound of the alarm, the ground floor became frantic. It was clear to Leo, rushing past, that no one knew what to do. Some stall holders scurried to secure their stock, while others continued to negotiate with passing customers. At one stall, Leo passed a man holding up outfits for the attention of two women wearing brightly coloured headscarves. At the next, a toddler tugged on his mother's arm whilst she finished a box of noodles.

There had to be a gas isolation valve somewhere. If he could turn that off it would stop any of the fire from getting started.

Heading for the back of the mall, Leo passed the security guard he had seen minutes before. The guard was now shouting at people to move. Then, Leo noticed, behind the place where the guard had been sitting, a small door. It was painted the same dirty light blue as the rest of the mall.

Walking towards the door, Leo checked the guard wasn't watching. He was arguing with a group of men on the other side of the mall who were intent on browsing phone cases despite the alarm. He wouldn't notice a thing.

Leo pulled open the door and stepped inside.

* * *

On the eighth floor, Yee still hadn't seen Jiao, Leo or Allissa. Had his mind been playing tricks on him? Had he been seeing things?

He had been so sure it was them.

His brief concern for the residents who continued to ignore the alarm had turned into a kind of pity. Yee had not seen any of them making their way out as they should. Although the alarm had disturbed their chores, rest or play, it was treated as an irritant rather than a concern.

There really was no helping some people.

Reaching the balcony, Yee scanned the apartment doors. He knew there was an apartment on this floor where a family had been evicted only days ago.

Which one was it?

All the doors were closed, no doubt to keep out the noise of the wailing alarm. All except one. That must be it. Jiao must be in there already.

* * *

Inside the apartment on the eighth floor, Jiao pulled the cooker from the wall. This was the tenth and final one.

Nine rooms were now filling with gas. In five minutes, nine devices would ignite it into beautiful, destructive, cleansing flames.

The alarm, which had initially concerned him, now reassured him. Both because he could see the residents ignoring it and because he knew he'd disconnected it from the network. It wouldn't call anyone to help.

286

Jiao knew that the fire service in Hong Kong took anywhere between ten and twenty minutes to respond. Within a few minutes of the first detonation the whole building would be on fire. There would be nothing anyone could do.

With a grin, he pulled the pipe from behind the cooker. Gas started to fill the room.

Chapter 98

"It's been in my family for three generations, it's worth a lot of money, no one knows how much. It can't just be replaced."

Allissa remembered Yee's voice as she picked up the ring from the floor. It was priceless, apparently. No wonder he was pissed off.

Smiling to herself, Allissa thought of Isobel on the plane to Kathmandu.

"Good girl," she whispered. She was surprised, shocked, but strangely impressed by Isobel's resolve to get revenge on Yee by stealing from him.

That girl will be alright, Allissa thought, tucking the ring into her pocket. They would decide what to do with it later, although Allissa doubted Yee would ever get it back.

Turning from the room and picking the bags up again, Allissa opened the door and headed back towards the balcony.

Outside the balcony was empty. People had either listened to the yelling alarm and left the building or closed their doors to try and block its noise.

There was only one door that was open and that was the door of the apartment next door. It was the door to the apartment from which the family had been evicted a few days before. The heavy chain lay open on one of the handles, the padlock dangling from the end.

Curiosity rising inside her, Allissa stepped towards it.

Why would that be open now?

* * *

As Leo's eyes adjusted to the light, he began to see the contents of the small room. It was essentially the control room of the building.

Two old, large TV screens flickered showing a dozen images from the CCTV cameras around the building. A desk occupied one corner, littered with dusty magazines. The two covers Leo could see showed scantily clad Chinese women pouting at the reader.

On the opposite wall, some kind of control system flashed intermittently beneath years of filth. And to the left, almost behind the door, two vertical pipes ran from the floor to the ceiling, one black, one red.

Leo looked at them closely. This could be it.

In the centre of both, large valves were buried beneath cobwebs.

Leo stepped across to the pipes and examined them. If one was the water main, then the other was what he was looking for, the building's gas valve. Turning this off could save the building from the inferno that Leo and Allissa had almost been part of in the restaurant the day before.

Chapter 99

On the eighth floor, Allissa peered through the gap in the door. Inside she saw two people she recognised immediately. The first, facing away from the door, was Yee. His grey-flecked hair was now out of place and he was shouting wildly at the larger man, who Allissa recognised as his assistant, Jiao.

Jiao looked at Yee but didn't stop what he was doing, pressing buttons on the device he was setting up next to the cooker.

Looking at the door Allissa made a decision.

Silently she pushed the door closed and threaded the chain back through the lock. Then, pulling the chain tight, she closed the padlock around it.

Give them a taste of their own medicine.

* * *

The valve was stiff as Leo tried to turn it. He'd assumed the smaller of the two pipes was the gas feed to the building.

Leo felt metal grinding against metal as he strained. The valve wasn't budging. He tried again. The sores on his hands from breaking the glass earlier stung.

He'd need something to help him. He looked around the room. Something that he could either hold the valve with, or thread through it for leverage.

In the shadow of the opposite corner, Leo saw an iron crowbar. The sort used for prising open doors when they were jammed.

That would do.

Crossing the room, Leo picked it up. It was solid.

Threading the thin end through the valve, he leaned down on the crowbar. With the added leverage, the valve crunched and began to turn. Leo repeated the process until it had done a full turn and jammed shut. The gas was off.

Glancing at one of the screens, Leo saw a fire engine pull up outside. It was time for them to get out.

Putting the crowbar back, Leo opened the door and peered out. The security guard was now arguing with one of the stall holders.

Ducking out of the room, Leo joined the throngs of people still ignoring the screaming alarm and walked towards the exit.

Chapter 100

Mya packs quickly, throwing the few things she needs into a small bag. She's not taking much – a clean set of clothes, passport, money, credit card. Just enough to get her off the island.

For a moment she stops and thinks about what she's doing. She thinks about Leo out on the jetty metres away. Then she thinks about the time they've spent together. The question he's just asked. Finally, she thinks about the man waiting for her outside.

Mya pulls the ring from her pocket and looks at it. The ring Leo has just given her. She makes a fist around it and holds it tight.

Maybe Leo deserves to know. Maybe she should try to explain. But he wouldn't get it, he wouldn't understand.

He will go back to Brighton, go back to his grey life in the drizzling city, and that's him. Just as much as that's not her.

Opening her hand and looking down at the ring again, its diamonds glinting fiercely in the light, Mya knows she's doing the right thing.

Placing it on the dressing table, she slips from the door of the cabin. Leo is still at the end of the jetty looking out to the sea. He's got his life, and she's got hers.

"I thought you weren't coming," a voice says as Mya walks down the path beside the cabin.

"I've got us a hotel on the other side of the island," he says. "We will stay there tonight and then we're on the boat to Samui at 6 a.m. You got everything?" He starts to walk up towards the main road. "There's a taxi waiting for us."

"Wait a sec," Mya says.

Leo stands from the end of the jetty and walks towards the land. Behind him the stars stretch out like a map, a universe of possibilities. Many of which he's yet to discover.

Black and white. Light and dark. Stay or go.

The night-time noise of the jungle swells. Somewhere a bat pounds the air, and an engine idles softly.

"Yeah, ready," Mya says. "Let's go,"

* * *

Five minutes must be up, Leo thinks, turning his back on the Kao Tao night. To arrive in Kao Tao with Mya has been incredible, one of the most completing experiences of his life.

The sound of the island intensifies around him. Two animals yammer somewhere far off. The sea and the sand breathe together in harmony and insects call to one another in the undergrowth.

Light from the window of the cabin they're staying in shimmers across the water.

Somewhere up the road a car starts, its engine whines for a moment before fading.

Reaching the cabin, Leo looks back out across the dark ocean and the map of stars spread above. Right now, on this beautiful island, waiting for the answer to the question of his life, Brighton feels like a million miles away.

"I'm coming in…" Leo says to the door.

Inside, she lies on the bed, facing away from him. He sees the curve of her back, the pinch of her waist, the swell of her bum. He knows what it's like to lie next to that body, to feel that woman next to him and he can't wait to spend the rest of his life doing it.

"You're full of surprises tonight," he says, sitting on the bed next to her.

She doesn't reply.

Then she turns.

Her skin is darker, her hair bigger, her eyes bright but different. Her smile is still intoxicating. But it's not Mya.

Chapter 101

L eo's eyes shot open. Until a moment ago he'd slept soundly on the giant bed in the comfort and safety of their hotel room, but something had disturbed his sleep. He couldn't work out what it was.

They'd checked in the day before, bedraggled, tired and sore after a ridiculous two days of not enough food or rest.

Usually in hotels, Leo and Allissa got a twin room. Last night the hotel didn't have one available and neither of them had the energy to discuss it.

They'd started the night on their separate sides of the giant bed, but now waking, Leo felt himself wrapped around Allissa's sleeping shape. Realising their closeness and feeling as though he was doing something he shouldn't, Leo rolled back to his own side. From there, he looked at Allissa. A feeling of warmth rose within him. To try and suppress it, Leo concentrated on trying to work out what time of the day it was. It looked like morning from the light piling through the blinds, but he couldn't be sure.

His mind and eyes wandered back to Allissa. He'd not been physically close with anyone since Mya had gone missing. The thought of it still made him uncomfortable. Current events had distracted him from looking for her, but he still felt that he owed something to their relationship. Finding out at least. And Leo knew that if he admitted the search for Mya was over, that would raise all sorts of questions in his friendship with Allissa.

Things are simple like this, he repeated to himself, *don't make them complicated.*

He was looking for Mya. He and Allissa were just friends.

But looking at Allissa again, he did have to admit, as he had always known, she was incredible.

Then Leo thought of the events of the previous day. They'd avoided death twice, saved one person's life and possibly countless more if Yee's plan of the fire in the flats had worked. Leo smiled. He wouldn't have done it without Allissa. In fact, as ever, he felt that she did more than he did.

It was amazing sometimes, Leo thought to himself in the silent room, how when two people work well together, the good they can do is not just added but multiplied. *She's incredible,* he thought again, forcing himself out of bed before the thought could develop any further. Then as some kind of penance, Leo crossed to their giant bathroom, put the shower on the coldest setting, stripped and stepped beneath it.

"I've just ordered breakfast," Allissa shouted as Leo turned off the shower a few minutes later. Hearing the mention of breakfast made him hungry.

Two English-style cooked breakfasts: bacon, eggs, sausage and baked beans. Served with coffee, orange juice and extra toast.

While finishing off the food, Leo looked on his phone for flights. There was one the following morning to London Heathrow.

"That's great, as there's one more thing we need to do,"

Allissa said. "Then we'll get that flight."

Leo looked at her uncomfortably. He had been afraid she was going to say something like that.

Chapter 102

Mrs Yee, returning from visiting family in Shenzen, drove her BMW towards the apartment block on Hong Kong's mid-levels. It had been a good journey; her two daughters had slept draped across the backseat throughout.

She looked up at the tower, dark against the dishcloth clouds threatening to wring above the city.

She didn't miss the place. Her brother had again suggested they move up to live with them. Her girls could go to school with their cousins and her family would be there for support and company.

Again, she'd declined – they had to return to Hong Kong. The girls needed their father and she needed her husband. She was used to ignoring the cracks of doubt which covered her mind like cobwebs.

A few years younger than her husband, Mrs Yee got married when she was only twenty and had their first child a year later. Before meeting Yee, she'd planned to go to university in the United States or Europe.

"You don't need to do that now," he'd said. "I'll look after us."

She often wondered what life would have been like if she

hadn't met him. Or what would have happened if she'd said no. If she'd followed her dream, rather than being part of his.

He was a good man, she thought. He *was* a good man. He'd never done anything wrong. He provided for her and their daughters. But that was where his influence ended. She didn't know what absorbed so much of his time. In a way she didn't want to.

Turning the final corner, the dark mouth of the underground car park ahead, Mrs Yee saw a man standing at the side of the road. He looked like a tourist. He looked lost. Seemingly, without thinking, he stepped into the street in front of the car. Mrs Yee applied the brakes just in time to avoid hitting him.

Absorbed in avoiding a collision, Mrs Yee didn't notice the woman approach the car window. Tapping on the glass, the woman smiled.

Mrs Yee lowered the glass. The smell of the city tumbled in – humidity, foliage, exhaust fumes.

"You're Mrs Yee aren't you?" the woman said.

How could she have known that?

"We've had dealings with your husband. He's done a few things I think you deserve to know about." She passed a brown envelope through the open window. "Obviously what you do is up to you, but I think you and your beautiful daughters deserve better."

Mrs Yee sat in the car holding the envelope as the woman walked away. She watched in the rear-view mirror as their reflections grew small against the city below. Somehow, she knew the contents of the package would be important. Something about the way the woman had spoken told her she was not wasting her time.

Still holding the envelope, Mrs Yee looked out at the residential district she'd called home for nearly ten years. People were at work. Children were at school. The other wives in the block would be out on one of their spa days or fulfilling some element of their beauty regime. She thought most of them to be fake or shallow.

Sliding a finger underneath the unsealed flap of the envelope, she tilted it up. A printed photograph slid out into her hand. It was of a girl, lying naked, looking directly at the camera.

For a few seconds, Mrs Yee stared at the picture wondering if she knew the girl. She didn't think she did. No memories came forward.

Then she realised why she had been given the picture. It had been taken in their bedroom. She would recognise it anywhere. The table lamps, the picture on the wall, the bed covers.

Yee wasn't in it. He didn't need to be. This woman was in their bed, their marital bed. The bed in which they lay every night. The place the girls came when they weren't feeling well or had nightmares. The place she comforted her daughters when their dad didn't return from work.

Then she noticed something that made her blood run cold. On the finger of the naked girl was the ring Yee had given her when he had proposed. It was supposed to be expensive. Priceless even. A family heirloom.

In the past she had thought of it as security. Whatever happened she'd be able to sell it if needed. And now this girl had it, this random girl he hardly knew.

Feeling the anger build, her vision began to blur, her hand closed around the envelope.

There was something else inside it. Putting the photo on the passenger seat, Mrs Yee tipped the envelope over. Into the palm of her hand slid the ring. Thousands of dollars in gold and diamonds. Her ticket home.

Without another thought and without looking back at her home of nearly ten years, Mrs Yee turned the car around.

Chapter 103

"Taking the ring and that picture was a great idea," Leo said as they made their way back down towards central Hong Kong Island. "That'll take some serious explaining."

The smell of the big-leaved trees had already been replaced by diesel fumes. The sound of birds singing had become idling engines and the hiss of wind through high wire fences.

"I knew Isobel wouldn't be the only victim," Allissa said. "His wife wouldn't leave him without reason and means, and we just gave her both."

"That was a stroke of genius. How did you get Isobel to go along with it?"

"It was her idea. She asked me to take it while we were in Yee's bedroom together. She's such a strong woman."

"He's lost a lot more than he knows," Leo said, thinking of Yee sitting in his expensive, austere office, only to come back to an empty apartment.

They were now tracing the route Leo had taken two days before on his way back from The Peak. It seemed so long ago now, so much had happened.

"There is something you totally should see while we're here," Leo said, taking Allissa by the wrist. She stopped and looked at him. Leo knew she wasn't into tourist spots, but the famous view from The Peak couldn't be missed and their flights weren't until tomorrow.

The taxi set off up the hill at speed, the driver knew the road and took each of the corners quickly. The road took a different route to the one Leo had walked. It circled the slope, twisting and turning back on itself, each time producing a new vista across the back of the island.

A few minutes later they stepped out into The Peak's unlikely shopping plaza and walked up a path away from the crowds. Hong Kong's famous skyline lay below.

The green lusciousness of the trees tumbled down towards the mid-levels where the buildings clung precariously to the slope. Behind them, the towers of central Hong Kong Island looked small. And behind that, the channel of water separating the island from Kowloon, glimmered lazily.

Allissa looked out towards it, hands on the railing in front of her.

"It's a nice city, to be fair," she said. "It's just a shame people keep trying to ruin these places for us."

"I know, you're right."

A group of girls next to them took a selfie.

Leo had promised himself that he would tell Allissa about the picture. Life was too short and dangerous for secrets.

Walking further up the hill, they found a bench.

When they were both sat down, Leo drew a deep breath and started to speak.

"Mya was here."

"When?"

"I'm not sure. At least few months ago."

"How do you know that? I thought you'd not got any leads

303

on her."

"The day we got to Pokhara I got a message from your dad. He sent me a picture of her taken here with Hong Kong in the background. He said if I told him where you were, he would give me information about Mya."

Allissa said nothing. She looked out at the view. The skyline of the city was now partially obscured by two tall, thin trees.

"Did you reply?" she asked after a while, turning to look at Leo.

"No. I'd gone through all that effort to find you, and you seemed like a really decent person. I couldn't betray you like that."

"You should have told me about it."

"I wanted to, but..." Leo stuttered, "I didn't tell you about it to start with. Then there was his prosecution and trial. I felt like you had enough to deal with. Then afterwards, it felt like if I told you you'd think I deceived you."

Leo couldn't judge Allissa's reaction; she said nothing, did nothing, just listened.

"Do you still want to find her?" she asked, finally, turning to look at him.

"Yeah, of course," Leo replied. "We've got unfinished business, I suppose. I want to know why she left. I want to know if I did anything wrong. I want to know if she's safe."

"Yeah of course," Allissa said, turning back to look at the city. Watching her, Leo felt a knot twist in his stomach. Since that morning, it had felt like they were living in a bubble where everything was good. They'd woken up together having finished the job. They'd eaten breakfast on the giant bed whilst Allissa flicked through TV channels.

It was as though things had changed. Things were just, *good*.

And now he was damaging that. Now he was bringing up the past Allissa had been working hard to forget.

"It's not that I love her anymore or anything. I don't think," Leo said, talking quickly. "It's... I just feel I want to know what happened. I need to know. You know if something is unexplained or unfinished..."

"Yeah, I understand." Allissa spoke without looking at Leo. The pair were silent for a minute.

"Do you still have the picture?" Allissa asked.

"Yeah, I deleted the message, but I still have the picture."

"Show me."

Now it was Leo's turn not to reply.

"I want to see the picture my dad sent you. Show me." Allissa turned to face Leo. As their eyes met, Leo knew he couldn't argue.

Unlocking his phone, he scrolled back through the saved pictures. There were pictures from previous cases, pictures of his family. Then, there it was. Eight months earlier. The blue sky, the city stretching out, the unknown faces, and Mya.

"Here," Leo said, making it full screen and passing it to Allissa.

"Which one is she?"

It hadn't occurred to Leo that Allissa didn't know what Mya looked like. Obviously, she knew about her, he'd talked about her on the first day they'd met. In fact, he doubted Allissa would have trusted him had he not bared his own story of loss. He had photos of Mya, but they were all stored away somewhere – there was no reason Allissa would have seen them.

Putting two fingers on the screen, Leo zoomed in on one of the people in the group. Mya's bright eyes and wide smile filled the screen.

"You're joking," Allissa said, looking up towards him as though expecting a punch line. "You're sure this is her?"

Leo looked again – it definitely was. He would recognise her anywhere. He'd spent years trying to find her in blurry photos. It was definitely her.

"Yeah, that's her, that's the picture your dad sent me. No idea how he got it."

There was a silence as Allissa looked at the photo again.

Hong Kong lay clear and subdued in front of them, as though listening for Allissa's response. The chaos a distant memory.

A group of people walked past, stopping further down the path for a photograph. That same world-famous photograph Allissa examined on the screen of Leo's phone.

Allissa broke the silence first.

"I've seen this girl."

Leo looked at Allissa.

"I've seen this girl in Hong Kong."

Chapter 104

Having served a lifelong apprenticeship in stories, watching sitcoms, films, soaps and reading widely, Leo felt he knew how to react in every situation that could arise. He'd learned the best way to tell someone your feelings from late nineties romantic comedies, even if you left it until the last moment. He knew how to deal with loss, projecting the necessary abject sadness into his expression and words. He felt like he knew how to passively disagree with someone to such an extent that it didn't upset them, or recover from an embarrassing misunderstanding.

In fact, it occurred to him, on the journey down from The Peak, that perhaps his generation were at a loss. Perhaps you chose your character from the cast of 'Friends' and just learned the lines for each and every event. There were over seven billion people on the planet and six characters to choose from – were you a Joey, Phoebe or Rachel?

With that in mind, had anything in the past ever really surprised him? Before visiting India, Leo knew what it would be like having seen the reaction of a brightly dressed retired politician being shown the slums of Mumbai. He already knew the mysteries of the Egyptian Pyramids from YouTube, and three different theories about who built Maccu Piccu.

Was there any point going there? Would visiting actually teach him any more than he already knew?

Was this going to be first situation in his life for which he was completely unprepared. Had he been let down by all the writers, film makers and TV producers of the last thirty years? Cursing them all, he thought of all the nonchalant relationship breakup comebacks, stupid private jokes and chat up lines he'd never use. But what could he do now? What should he say? Had he missed, 'The One Where Chandler Finds His Missing Girlfriend'?"

As Allissa turned the corner into the street where the café was, Leo stopped. He had no idea how to go on. If it was her, what would he do? If it wasn't her what would he do?

How would Allissa feel? Why was he worried about Allissa's feelings?

If it was her, would seeing her bring back painful emotions he had already healed from?

What if it wasn't her, would he be disappointed?

Did he even want it to be her?

Leo stood on the corner of the street, the busy throng of Nathan Road behind him. Shoppers carried glossy bags from one store to the next and spoke excitedly in a multitude of languages. Despite the noise, Leo didn't hear anything.

Allissa walked on, not noticing that Leo had stopped.

Ahead, the Serendipity Café looked quiet. Leo watched Allissa look left and right for him, then stop. He saw her, the woman he had woken up next to that morning, the woman he had secretly enjoyed waking up next to, stop walking and turn to face him.

Leo's loss through Mya had taken him to Kathmandu, events in Kathmandu had connected him to Allissa, and now their expertise had brought them to Hong Kong. Was it so hard to believe that Mya would be here as well? The world was only so big.

Taking a few steps back, Allissa reached out, took Leo's hand and together they crossed the road.

Chapter 105

Mya flicked through the TV channels in the Serendipity Café. She was being paid by the hour but getting older by the minute.

On the screen, a pack of tigers picked meat from the bones of a carcass.

She had been in Hong Kong nine months, ending up in the city after running out of money to keep going. The guy she was travelling with didn't want to wait, so he carried on without her. They had seen a few places together. It had been fun but didn't last.

The café was quiet, the lunchtime rush long since finished but they were still hours from closing. Then after work she was going out again, seeing a band playing somewhere.

Mya flicked the channel. A news reader spoke silently to the camera. The report cut to footage showing guns being fired and children crying.

Hong Kong was supposed to be temporary; Mya was saving money to make her next move to Singapore, Indonesia and Australia. She knew someone in Brisbane. She was supposed to be saving anyway, but all these nights out were becoming expensive.

On the next channel Mya watched a man throw a glass of

wine over a woman, the aggression of their argument lost without the sound.

The door jangled as a customer came into the café.

On the screen the man and woman continued to argue, human existence reduced to one banal conflict.

Drums pounded in Leo's ears as he looked at the woman he had spent two years searching for. Leaning on the counter, her chin in her palm, Leo knew it was Mya instantly. It had to be.

Looking at him as she turned, she dropped the remote control. It clattered to the counter.

Leo didn't move. Mya stared towards him open mouthed.

Neither said anything for a few long seconds. Allissa watched from the doorway.

"Hi," Leo said, finally, realizing someone had to say something.

Mya shook her head, as though resetting her thoughts.

"Hello," she said, brightly. "This is a real surprise. I... I... What are you doing here?"

Leo didn't reply, considering Mya through narrowed eyes.

"How... How long have you been in Hong Kong?"

He wasn't doing small talk.

"Let's get a table," he said, pointing towards the corner.

"I really should stay," Mya pointed towards the counter. "In case we have customers."

Allissa stepped back towards the door, flipped the sign to closed and twisted the lock.

"This really won't take that long," Leo said.

Watching Mya follow them to the table in the corner, Leo felt detached from himself. If anything, he felt emotionless. Like he was looking at the world through someone else's eyes.

Mya sat across the table from them.

"Two years I've been looking for you," Leo said, his voice deep and monotone. "Two years every night I'd come home from work and I'd look for you. Go through newspapers, pictures, forums, anything that might be you."

Mya looked up at him, her wide eyes glistening.

"I wanted to tell you," Mya said, her fingers dancing across the table.

Leo didn't reply.

"I wanted to. I couldn't find the words. I didn't know how."

"So you just ran away? You let me think you were missing or dead?"

"That night, it was so hard to leave you, but I couldn't go back with you. I knew that. I wanted to tell you. To say something. But then you asked me to..." She breathed hard. "Then you gave me that ring. I just couldn't do that. That was totally not my life. I couldn't go back to Brighton and just do nothing..."

Leo moved his hands together on the table. Mya looked just as he had remembered; dark hair, slender neck, wide bright eyes that used to absorb him completely.

"I get that, I think," Leo said. "But you needed to tell me. What you did was cruel."

Mya looked at her hands.

"We just weren't..." Mya trailed off. "It just wasn't what I wanted. What I needed."

"I looked for you," Leo said again, knitting his hands together. "For two years. For two years. Every day I would sit at my computer and try to find clues about where you'd gone. I thought you'd been kidnapped... or worse."

"I know, I felt so bad afterwards. I'm sorry."

"No, you're not, and even if you were, I wouldn't care." Leo felt anger rising. "You meant something to me. However hard it was to have that conversation, you should have done that."

"I wrote you loads of letters," Mya said, sniffing, "but could never send them. They just didn't sound right."

"I'm sure," Leo said, his breath becoming tight. "I was so…" He stopped. Each breath tighter than the last.

The rising panic absorbing his thoughts.

Breathe in and out.

This is what Mya did to him. She'd done this for years and was still doing it.

Calm, focus, breathe.

How could she…

Breathe in and out.

Mya watched Leo silently as he tried to focus.

Calm, focus, breathe.

Breathe in and out.

Then Leo felt Allissa's hand on his arm.

Through the tempest of his anger he remembered what Allissa had said to Isobel two days ago.

"If we were in your situation, we'd have done the same thing."

Leo realized, for the first time, he was in control. The choice was his, he could choose to hate, or forgive. He could choose to destroy or unite. He could choose order or chaos.

"I did, I thought about you… I'm… I'm…" Mya said.

Calm, focus, breathe.

Leo looked up at Mya, the eyes he'd wanted to see for so long. The woman that he thought for years would bring him solace.

Calm and focus.

He took a moment to calm himself. Swallowing his anxiety,

Leo looked directly at Mya. She was just a person. She had no control over him. The only thing that gave her power was Leo himself.

The choice was his.

Breathe in, and out.

He was in control.

Calm and focus.

Calm.

Leo exhaled slowly.

"It's okay," he said. "You did what you did, and I did what I did. I'm glad you're alright."

Mya looked back at him blankly.

"It's been nice to see you because there was still a part of me that worried about you. I did wonder where you'd gone and why you didn't want to be found. But now I can put that to rest. I suppose I just wanted to have the conversation that you didn't think was important."

With that Leo got to his feet.

"I'm going to go now because there's lots of people who need my help. And we've got a flight to catch."

Leo walked to the door. Allissa followed.

Mya said nothing. Watching Leo, her eyes sparkled.

At the door Leo paused, turned and looked back at Mya. For the last time he saw the lips he had hoped to kiss again. The eyes he had longed to stare into. But the woman who stared back at him wasn't the woman he wanted. It wasn't the Mya he had known those years ago, or the Mya he had longed to see again. She was just another person. Yes, a person he had once loved, but one that he now had nothing more to say to.

He had good memories of her, but that's all they were.

"We have to go home," Leo said, raising a hand in a wave. Then, looking from Mya to Allissa, he stepped out into the bright afternoon.

In the street he didn't look back. Allissa walked beside him, and neither spoke until the café was out of sight.

"We're the good guys," Allissa said, breaking the silence. "There's too many people in the world that'll be nasty to each other. We're here to balance that out."

Leo stopped walking and looked at Allissa. People darted left and right to avoid them on the busy street.

Somewhere in the world a tiger ate a lamb, a soldier marched towards a child who couldn't see for tears and a man threw a drink at a woman. A billion years of evolution and it's not the acts themselves that are frightening, but their perpetual repetition. Somewhere else though, old friends are reunited, a child says their first words and on a street in Hong Kong, a man with a free heart pulls a woman close.

For a moment Leo nestles his face into Allissa's shoulder and smells the coconut he's become so fond of. Then he pulls back and looks at her. *It's entropy*, is what he would have thought if his mind wasn't cluttered with questions and desires. Watching Allissa's lower lip curl beneath her teeth, he realizes what he's been fighting for so long. *We're battling against the world's ability to pull things apart and level them out*, Leo thinks, leaning in.

"Come on," Allissa said, breaking off the hug with a hand on Leo's chest. "We've got work to do."

BERLIN

Leo and Allissa's next case will take them to one of my favourite European cities – Berlin. At the time of writing

(November 2019) I'm nearing the end of the first draft.

Berlin will be a little different though. For the first two weeks of its release it will be available as an eBook exclusively and free of charge to those who support me through my mailing list. There'll be a heavy discount for paperbacks too, but for obvious reasons I can't give these away for nothing!

I'm doing this because my favourite part of publishing *Kathmandu* earlier this year was talking to the people who have read and enjoyed it. Before sharing my work, I didn't realise that I only write the story – it comes to life when you guys read it. So, *Berlin* will be for you.

It'll be ready in the first few months of 2020 and I'd love for you to get a copy. If you're not already, get on my mailing list now and I'll keep you informed.

www.LukeRichardsonAuthor.com/mailinglist

Dedication

As always, this book is dedicated to those I travel beside. Especially Jon, Helen, James and Alex. Through you I'm rediscovering the adventure of childhood.

Thank you

Thank you for reading *Hong Kong*. Sharing my writing with you has been a dream of many years. Thank you for making it a reality.

As may come across in my writing, travelling, exploring and seeing the world is so important to me. As is coming home to my family and friends.

Although the words here are my own, the characters, experiences and some of the events described are wholly inspired by the people I've travelled beside. If we shared noodles from a street-food vendor, visited a temple together, played cards on a creaking overnight train, or had a beer in a back-street restaurant, you are forever in this book.

It is the intention of my writing to show that although the world is big and the unknown can be unsettling, there is so much good in it. Although some of the people in my stories are bad and evil – the story wouldn't be very interesting if they weren't – they're vastly outnumbered by the honesty, purity and kindness of the other characters. You don't have to look far to see this in the real world. I know that whenever I travel, it's the kindness of the people that I remember almost more than the place itself. Whether you're an experienced traveller, or you prefer your home turf, it's my hope that this story has taken you somewhere new and exciting.

Despite the best efforts of me and my team, mistakes will

always creep through. If your eagle eyes have picked any out, please let me know at Hello@LukeRichardsonAuthor.com and I'll get them changed straight away.

Again, thank you for coming on the adventure with me, I hope to see you again.

Luke

PS. A little warning, next time someone talks to you in the airport, be careful what you say, as you may end up in their book.

Book reviews

If you've enjoyed this book, I would really appreciate you leaving a review.

www.LukeRichardsonAuthor.com/reviews

Reviews are so important as they encourage people who've never heard of me to take a risk on a first-time author. The bookselling websites also use them to decide what books to recommend to their customers. They really are like gold dust to an author!

It will take you no longer than two minutes and will mean the world to me.

Thank you.